THE PARIS HAT

The Paris Hat

By MARY CUNNINGHAM

FUNK & WAGNALLS, NEW YORK

Contents

THE PARIS HAT

1

Riddle of the Golden Heart

WHENEVER CATHY THOUGHT of the miracle that was going to happen at five o'clock, she had to cross her arms over her chest to keep her heart from leaping right out with excitement. There were moments, too, when the excitement seemed to settle in her legs, making them so wobbly that she wondered whether she'd be able to dance at all when Rex came—at five o'clock.

The very idea that Rex, who at eighteen had been dancing professional ballet for a year, would even notice her at the year-end folk-dance festival, let alone ask her to dance with him, was so overwhelming that it had a misty, almost unreal quality.

Part of the excitement, too, was due to the strangeness of being with her sister Bettina at Aunt Faith's big, quiet house for a two-week summer holiday, away from the hectic hullabaloo of home among their four brothers and sisters who were now at camp near Mount Diablo. Having a goal was another part of the excitement—a goal as dazzling as it had been unthinkable a week ago. But ever since Rex had come into her life, she was sure that she, also, wanted to be a professional ballet dancer.

There were nearly three hours to wait before Rex would arrive, but she stood at the open front door expectantly, Bettina beside her, looking into the buoyant, blue and gold, windy, clear brightness that was San Francisco's June.

Bettina sighed. "I wish I could quit being twelve and leap ahead about four years so that thrilling things like Rex would happen to me."

Just hearing his name spoken sent music ringing brightly through Cathy's head—a soft bird song, hung on a shaft of wind-washed air, part of the music inside her, part of the special happiness that seemed arched over everything today. And in a lightning flash she was reliving that last day at school when the miracle had happened, when Rex had made this date to come for their first dance practice together.

"Hero worship," Miss Allison, Cathy's gym teacher, had called it. For a moment Cathy's whole train of thought about Rex halted to let in Miss Allison's odd little speech of warning and encouragement. She had quoted her favorite slogan: "Set your sights high, but face your limitations squarely." Puzzled, Cathy still didn't see how this applied to her. All this year the most popular girls at school had been bubbling over with plans for careers—plans dramatic and daring, plans to be envied when you were up to your ears in a prosaic job of looking after five younger brothers and sisters. Doctor Darfield's motherless brood, the neighbors called them. And now magically all that was changed.

"Oh, it's so wonderful to know where I'm going," she

told Bettina. "It's wonderful—wonderful—wonderful!" Her voice involuntarily shaped to the lift of secret delight, and the shimmering longing to dance was so strong in her that all at once Miss Allison was just a hazy speck back in the school gym office, and Cathy's slim, straight legs whirled her out on the porch in a pirouette.

The reverberations of an unseen jet plane overhead in the bright blue sky seemed to catch her up and pull her farther and farther into the newness and wonder of another world. Touched by the same enchantment the pleated navy skirt swirled and became the ruff of an exquisite gauzy *tutu,* white and lovely, that she would wear when she and Rex danced in a rainbow of footlights. The roar of applause was sweet in her ear and the whole picture in a high key of exaltation. Then it was shattered rudely as Bettina said, "We could take our bikes and ride through Golden Gate Park to eat up the hours till five. That ought to limber your legs even better than all those funny exercises you call *pliés.*"

But Cathy couldn't answer. Legs stilled, arms abruptly pressed into her ribs, her astonished gaze was riveted on a smartly uniformed delivery boy, who had jumped out of a smart-looking truck at the curb. A golden splash of sunlight seemed to focus on a huge heart-shaped box he carried. As both girls watched spellbound, he glanced again at the house number to check the address and then bounded up the steps and handed the box to Cathy. A merry salute, and away he went in his shiny truck, leaving Cathy with the momentary feeling that in some eerie way her own thumping heart had really jumped out of her skin and landed in her arms. Mingled with the eerie feeling, the mystery, was a faint forewarning, as though something in this golden-heart box, with its extravagant ribbon ties of wide, cherry-red satin, spoke of complications to come.

"It's a valentine—a valentine," Bettina shrieked, finding her voice.

"It can't be. It isn't anywhere near Valentine's day," Cathy pointed out.

Bettina fingered the ribbon. "Golly, it's big and high enough for an elephant's heart."

Going back into the house, Cathy studied the label—*Chapeaux de Paris.* "Hats of Paris," she translated for Bettina. But it must be a mistake.

Bettina gasped. "Faith would never buy a Paris hat."

"But her name's on the address tag. Mrs. Patrick Mc-Queen, 321 Scenic Circle, San Francisco." Still, Cathy knew Bettina was right. There was no more sense in Faith's getting a Paris hat in a glamorous golden heart than there would have been for Jimbo, her black spaniel, to get a pair of Spanish side combs. Faith was lovely to look at, terribly sweet, and so young that they had never even considered calling her "Aunt," and yet there was something odd about her. Her clothes were lovely, but she never seemed interested in them. You had the feeling that she must have bought them long ago. "But it can't be too long ago," Cathy said, thinking out loud. "She's only twenty-six."

Bettina asked incredulously, "No one would ever send Faith a present like this, would they?"

"No, of course not." Yet, here it was. "It makes you begin to think of Faith in a whole new way, doesn't it?" At the same time Cathy realized that for a long while she'd felt nothing about her young aunt at all. There was a strange, locked-up far-awayness that gave Faith a kind of disembodiment and left a smooth hollow in the back of Cathy's mind through which Faith's name floated.

"Oh, I wish I could remember!" Cathy squeezed her

gray eyes shut in a compelling effort to recall some tantalizing bits of family talk about Faith and another Paris hat in the past. But the bits wouldn't come together into any kind of real memory that made sense, and when Cathy opened her eyes again, there was Cora, Faith's maid, heaving toward them down the hall.

"Look! Look!" Bettina shrieked, snatching the box from Cathy and thrusting it at Cora.

It was easy to understand that Cora would be astonished, but when her eyes just about fell out of her big, round face and she began twisting her freshly starched apron as though something in the box had reached out and grabbed her, the whole riddle of the box became more bewildering than ever. This was particularly true because the whole bulgy two hundred and ten pounds of Cora's solid, common-sense comfortableness had always seemed able to deal with anything.

"What does it mean?" Bettina demanded, jumping up and down like a black-banged pixie.

But every line of Cora's great bulk in its blue uniform seemed petrified with shock, and then a choked, gurgling noise began to rumble up out of her immense bosom, ending in a faint, "Oh, blessed heaven! I hope it'll work this time."

Now what did that mean? But before Cathy could add her question to Bettina's bubbling clamor, Faith herself came in. For the first time Cathy noticed how Faith's fragile slenderness gave a special air of elegance to her Red Cross uniform. The cap of her uniform was under her arm, and Cathy could tell that she had been on her favorite walk along the brook in Sutro Forest because her pale-blond hair was wind-blown and she carried a bunch of the little mist maidens that grew in the shady moistness along the trail.

There was a great flurry of black fur down the hall and a low growl of delight as Jimbo flung himself in ecstatic greeting against Faith's legs.

"You've got another Frenchy hat, ma'am," Cora cried. She took a crackling, starched step forward as though she expected her young mistress to need holding up, but Faith just stood there perfectly still. The leafy light from the open door made queer lacy shadows on the white of her face, as white and affecting as the delicate mist maidens in her hand. She seemed to be looking deep, deep into the box, seeing what was inside without opening it. Cathy knew that the golden heart had brought a message, one that Faith and Cora both understood. Yet, it had taken them by surprise—a surprise that was nice, perhaps, but perhaps frightening, too, with the same forewarning she herself had felt.

And then her thoughts circled back to Rex, to the melting in her knees, to the strange thrust of panic, which she sensed now repeated in Faith. A brief glimpse of herself in the hall mirror brought back his words: "You've got the right figure for a dancer: long legs, lightly boned, a strong supple back." Oh, she was strong. She was, indeed. She strained toward the mirror again, oblivious of the scene around her, looking for outward signs of this new strength. Was she really strong enough, determined enough, to reach her goal undistracted? She saw only a slender, long-legged girl with a serious oval face, the faint dusting of freckles that went with coppery hair, dark-lashed gray eyes that were asking, asking. . . . She turned from the mirror to the room that was full of another kind of asking.

Cathy swallowed hard in sympathy because Faith's obvious compound of delight and anxiety was identical with what she had been feeling about Rex.

She could sense that Bettina, with her penchant for an overdose of drama, was simply popping with questions. Her mouth opened for one to come out but closed again at a silencing glance from Cora. Then they were herded out to the kitchen. As the door was closed behind them, Bettina exploded, "Tell us, Cora, what does it mean? The heart box and the hat?"

Cora cut three wide slices of jelly roll, motioned to the girls to help themselves. It seemed as though she was stuffing her own mouth to keep from talking. Of course, she was always stuffing herself, anyway. Everyone knew Cora was the world's most fabulous cook, and since everything she made was so irresistible, she just couldn't stop eating. She had a way of grabbing quick bites with one hand while the other did something else, as she was doing now with one hand kneading dough for citron buns.

Bettina sighed. "Maybe it isn't a hat in the box after all."

This was bait, and Cora fell for it. "It's a hat, right enough."

"But who sent it?" Cathy urged.

Cora said, "I'm not one to go blabbing stuff to kids."

"Kids!" Bettina hooted. "Cathy's going to be seventeen in two weeks. She's even got a career all planned."

"Career?" Cora caught at the word. Her huge dough-kneading arm in its starched uniform sleeve crackled to a stop. "What career is that?"

"Haven't you noticed how she's been making like a ballet dancer every day?" Bettina's small, blue-jeaned legs went into a quick imitation of Cathy's limbering-up exercises.

Cathy squirmed. Although some of her happiest moments these last few days had been spent in this big spicy kitchen with Cora, and Cora herself was the essence of jolly coziness, still, ballet seemed completely out of her sphere and made Cathy feel unaccountably shy.

"Ballet." Cora shook her head dubiously. "Did I ever tell you about my niece Bessie?"

This side excursion in the conversation, Cathy knew, wasn't purely to divert attention from Faith. When Cora launched into the adventures of her far-flung circle of nephews and nieces, nothing could stop her. It was family legend that there was always a niece or a nephew whose experience was apropos of the subject of the moment.

"Bessie took up the high fandango on an elephant's back for the circus," said Cora. "We were all there, proud as you please, to see her opening night; but the fool elephant tripped going into the ring and sprained his ankle. Swole up the size of a bass drum, it did, quicker'n you could snap your fingers." Cora's snapping fingers produced a floury shower over the table.

"So what did Bessie do then?" Bettina persisted.

"Oh, her boy friend, a nice, steady milkman, stepped in and married her, and now they're settled down happy as clams with two sets of twins."

"Two?" Bettina's eyes rolled. Cora wrenched off a piece of dough with a businesslike twist and gave Cathy a nod which said plainly, "Let Bessie be a lesson to you."

"Only, I'm not dancing with an elephant." Cathy laughed aloud as the absurd picture of Bessie collided with thoughts of Rex.

"She's dancing with a boy who's about the best ballet dancer in all San Francisco. Anyway," Bettina went on, dusting crumbs of jelly roll from her small pointed chin, "if Cathy's old enough to be working on this career, and everyone knows she's been looking after all of us for three years—ever since Mama died—she's certainly old enough to know about this Paris hat that Faith got."

If any argument could bring Cora around, this ought to do it, Cathy decided. One of ten children herself, Cora had done what she called a powerful lot of minding of kids in her own teens, and her sympathy for Cathy, with Dad away most of the time and only old Mee Chow, their Chinese cook, to help, was limitless.

But surprisingly she said only, "By the way, Cathy's Walt phoned this morning before you girls were up."

"You make Walt sound like he's Cathy's personal property," Bettina protested.

Cathy smiled ruefully to herself. "Cathy's Walt" was the way the whole family had him pegged. Of course, it was nice that Dad and Grandma and all the aunts and uncles liked Walt. And after all he was her oldest and best friend. His brash self-confidence, his contagious enthusiasm for all his crazy inventions, his cream-colored crew cut loomed up as familiarly as home and the well-worn path between her house and his. But that wasn't saying there wasn't room for somebody else—someone like Rex. If only the family knew a little more about ballet!

Bettina was helping Cora shape the buns, and the words she tossed over her shoulder registered with a sickening clutch. "Walt's coming over later. But don't worry. He won't be here to bother you and Rex. He's coming after dinner."

Cathy relaxed. The thought of the dropped-jaw amazement, not to mention the frank comments she could imagine Walt delivering if he happened in on their practice period, died a welcome death.

"He's coming to see *me*, anyway," Bettina informed her with portent. "I'm doing some research for him."

"What kind of a contraption is he tinkering on now?" Cora asked.

Bettina's chest under its strawberry-striped shirt swelled with importance. "It isn't exactly an invention this time. It's more of an *idea* to make money. He's been saving a college fund for four years, but each year his folks get in some desperate state, like his father's burst appendix last winter, and he has to start all over. What he needs is capital. Capital," she informed Cora loftily, "is a big hunk of money that you can lean back on and let work for you. Golly, that sounds nice, doesn't it?" She paused, momentarily charmed by the literal idea.

"Of course, he's got a summer job," Cathy put in. "He's down at a riding academy in Burlingame."

"Which he's wonderful at, because horses just naturally behave when they're with him," Bettina, so obviously Walt's devoted slave, rushed on. "And now he's got this really terrific new idea." Then, in response to Cathy's mystified inquiry, "Didn't I tell you he was over here yesterday while you were out buying those new ballet slippers?"

Further information was cut short by the ringing of the doorbell. Cora gave a hasty smooth to her apron, and Cathy felt her pulse quicken. Had Rex come early?

But it wasn't Rex. It was their cousin Gerry, whose new yellow convertible was standing out front. And to their united astonishment there was Faith, just as they had left her in the hall, still standing and staring at the hatbox as though she were under a spell. Jimbo waited protectingly beside her.

"Now we'll find out," Bettina whispered to Cathy. "Gerry couldn't be mysterious about anything if she wanted to."

Gerry was a grown-up edition of Bettina, hair and eyes

black as licorice whips, a complexion of smooth, buttered-
toast tan, and a whole being so full of sparkle and bouncy
energy that just looking at her made you feel good. Cathy
thought Gerry would pounce on the box, put the hat on
her head, and go prancing into the living room. But it
wasn't like that at all. She just took a startled look at the
golden box and said with a tremulous up note, "Oh—oh,
Faith, sweet—"

Cora said, "It just came, Miss Geraldine." Even Cora's
common-sense voice was hushed and unnatural. Faith's
smile was like a dim light. Her eyes looked past them and
said nothing. But the hall was chock-full of the questions
they were all holding back. Then there was the soft,
muffled sound of Faith's steps on the rug as she picked up
the box. Cathy knew she would never forget the way
Faith put her hand under the cherry-red ribbon, as though
the touch was something she'd been waiting for, needing.
When they heard the click of Faith's door upstairs, all
Gerry's snap came back to her. "Can you beat that,
Cora?" she said.

"I won't deny I'm glad, Miss Geraldine," Cora said.

"Glad!" Gerry swooped Bettina and Cathy together
in a bracelet-jangling hug of high spirits. "Why, it's the
most exciting thing that's happened in years. And to think
I just whizzed by in time to get in on it! Matter of fact,
I was out on a business call and I thought I'd take these
two back to my office and then to Chinatown for dinner."

Gerry's office was a big, bustling advertising agency on
Market Street, where she was assistant art director, a
position that her brother Richard said was a ghastly stroke
of luck, because no man would ever propose to a girl
whose salary would probably be double his right from
the start. But certainly Gerry had all the dates any one
girl could look after, and no one ever noticed her worry-

ing about proposals—or about anything else, for that matter. Right now she seemed ready to forget all about the office to trail Cora back to the kitchen, a slim, tanned arm around each of the girls. Gerry perched on the edge of the kitchen table. "How long is it since he left the last time, Cora?" she asked.

Cora threw a thick green crescent of citron on the cutting board and said, "Two years last month, Miss Geraldine."

"That long! You know, he really has his nerve, hasn't he?"

Cora's knife slashed the citron—really slashed—she was so abruptly furious. "Call it that if you like."

"Oh, I forgot," Gerry said, "that you think the world of Pat. But you'd give a right arm for Faith, too, wouldn't you?"

With the mention of Uncle Pat's name, bits of family talk that Cathy had been trying to recall suddenly fell into place, and she eagerly followed what Gerry and Cora were saying. But it still didn't explain Cora's fury.

"How long was it after he sent the hat before he came home the last time?" Gerry wanted to know.

"That same day," Cora answered, sniffling.

"That means he may be here today," Gerry squealed. "Perhaps any minute!"

With Gerry's words a whirlwind of apprehension seemed to catch up Cathy and toss her dizzily round and round. Oh, no! she wanted to protest. Please, not right now when Rex is coming! Not now! Everything's happening too fast. Then the whirlwind set her down again, fiery-faced with shame. Her cold hand went up to push the hair from her hot forehead, as though she might push away the selfish thought that Faith shouldn't have all the nice things come to her just as fast as possible, because, all at once, she knew that Faith had been very unhappy.

While Gerry had been talking, her quick artist's fingers pushed cubes and slivers of citron into cunning designs on top of the buns. She looked like a little girl, her mouth puckered in concentration. Then suddenly she sat up straight, her black-velvet eyes simply alive with anticipation. "What will Faith do? What will Grandma say?" She turned to Cathy in her gay, darting way. "Go phone Grandma and tell her to get here as fast as she can. Tell her Faith's just gotten another Paris hat."

"But you know Grandma won't get up to answer the phone if she's settled herself to read in bed," Bettina pointed out.

Cathy's gaze flicked up to the Dutch clock over the stove. There was still a lot of time before Rex would be there. "Betts and I could run over and tell Grandma," she offered. And the next moment she and Bettina were racing out of the house and heading for the short cut over the hill that was all a wild tangle of dogwood and mountain lilac. When they came to their favorite spot, the hideaway in the thorn apple thicket, they stopped for breath.

Bettina panted, "What's it all about, Cathy? You know, don't you?"

"It's Uncle Pat, Faith's husband. Remember?"

Bettina's head bobbed up and down. "Of course. I remember how he played the piano. I remember how he took us on that lovely boat ride up Russian River on the Fourth of July, and he told us to close our eyes and make believe we were sailing a white canoe with a lantern of fireflies. It was a poem, I think. Oh, and I remember how he took us to the football game at Kezar Stadium. But he went away. What's the Paris hat got to do with it?"

"Well," Cathy explained, trying hard to remember exactly, "Faith and Uncle Pat went abroad on their honeymoon, and she brought home a Paris hat. Then almost right away Uncle Pat went into the Air Force, and when he was coming home, he sent her another Paris hat—to let her know they were going on another honeymoon, I guess."

"Then did he have to go back to the Air Force?"

"No, he went to Africa to look after some business about a diamond mine. And then he just had one thing and another to do, I imagine, because it's two years now." Cathy paused while nudged memory dredged up another detail. "Actually Uncle Pat wanted Faith to go with him, but she couldn't make up her mind. She was afraid, I guess."

"Afraid of cannibals?" Bettina demanded.

Cathy smiled. "All of Africa isn't full of cannibals. No, I think she was just afraid of going so far from home. You know how shy she is. So Uncle Pat went by himself. Only, no one had any idea he'd stay so long. The grownups feel it's kind of a disgrace. They're always very hush-hush, as though it was top secret stuff. Anyway, now he's coming home again—I guess—because—here's another Paris hat," she wound up with puzzled slowness.

"Is it like a present you send when you've been bad and want to make up?" Bettina asked.

"Maybe," Cathy decided, "it's more like a signal."

"That sounds nice." Bettina wriggled with delight and gave Cathy her up-tilted smile that was so exactly like their cousin Gerry's. "It's going to be fun—fun—fun! having Uncle Pat home again." She extended an arm for inspection. "Look! I'm all over goose pimples big as radishes. Remember that time he tipped the Fleishhacker Zoo man to show us the brand-new tiger cubs and the time we went camping over in Marin and he toasted marshmallows with me in the middle of the night because I couldn't sleep?" Bettina ran out of breath.

A painful lump caught in Cathy's throat as she remembered something else—the night Mama had died and Cathy had been worn out comforting the children and getting them to bed. Dad had closed the door to his room. Uncle Pat had taken her in his lap as though she weighed no more than a bean bag, and a cherishing hand had smoothed her hair and given her his big handkerchief.

Cathy was unaware of the pure joy that lighted her face with the next stab of memory. Uncle Pat and Faith had taken her to the only real ballet she had ever seen— "The Nutcracker." The wild, sun-dusted hillside blurred, and fragments of the Snow Queen's dance drifted magically before her eyes again. Her heart was beating now at a bursting pace with sudden revelation—why, Uncle Pat was the one person in the whole family circle who would fully and truly understand her dream of becoming a dancer. He'd understand Rex's artistic temperament, too, and be the ideal person to persuade Dad to let her study ballet seriously with a really good teacher.

When two things happened at once like this, synchronizing so perfectly, like Uncle Pat and Rex arriving on the same day, it must be a sign that there was a purpose behind it all. For a fleet second Cathy was shaken with awesome wonder; the soaring pressure of happiness sent her arms up in an airy gesture and her feet into the small, twinkling, even steps of a *pas de bourrée,* ending in the nearest approach to an *entrechat* she could manage.

Intrigued, Bettina tried to copy, but the result was a mad entanglement of arms and legs, and they went down together on the grassy ground in a gale of giggles.

"Oh, Cathy, I do love being *us* when you're *you!*"

"Silly!" Cathy said. "I'm me all the time." She scrambled to her feet.

"No, you're not. You've been someone else ever since —well, ever since you met Rex." Bettina's dark eyes blinked.

The woebegone look and the reproach in Bettina's voice stung Cathy. The quick denial died on her tongue. She turned away, brushing leaves from her clothes. "I *am* different, I guess," she admitted slowly. She was. She was! There was no denying the strange new power, the drive, the being-someone-special feeling.

The stranglehold of Bettina's small, wiry arms clasping her in a rush of entreaty made Cathy gasp for air. "Oh, Cathy, I wish you could be a terrific ballerina and be the old you, too."

Instinctively Cathy's capable hand moved in comfort on Bettina's back. It'll never work out, the realist Cathy told herself despairingly. Her head dropped down on Bettina's, coppery brown on Gypsy black, as they clung together. "Oh, Betts, Betts!" she murmured. How could she be the old Cathy to her brothers and little sisters when preparing for a career meant hours and hours of daily practice, fencing lessons, pantomime, acrobatics, toe work? "Why, I'll be lucky to just squeeze in my schoolwork," she thought, as she tried to strain out the sound of Bettina's voice going on and on.

"Who's going to look after us? You're the only one who can make Tess do her arithmetic and keep the twins' beetle collection corralled. And how about trouble at school and all our birthday parties? And you know how Pipper's always mashing a thumb or falling out of his tree house or something."

Cathy tried not to think of that after-school routine. Her sigh melted into the wind that stirred in the aromatic pine tree high over them. As a moment ago she had seen the Snow Queen's dancing in her mind's eye, now she saw Rex's lean face, so burnished, dark, the breath-taking beauty of his dancing, the controlled splendor of his leaps, the unforgettable moment when he had taken her hand, asking her to dance. She lived again the moment of panic, then the magical way her feet had gone along as he improvised. Poised there on that pinnacle of ecstatic remembering, she dared to think "maybe I've got more talent than I ever realized; maybe I can just rush through to a career and do everything else, too." If you wanted something enough, there had to be a way. You had to make a way. Her shoulders straightened. She took Bettina's hand. "Come on," she said, "we've got to hurry. "We've got to get to Grandma's and then home again as fast as we can."

2

Secret Dreams

GRANDMA WAS IN BED with a book. She always said that she was so old that if she wanted to read in bed around the clock, she guessed she could without the family saying boo. But when she heard about the hat, it was as though someone had sneaked up behind her and shouted boo through a trumpet. She gave a violent huff, her gaunt old white-hawk face sort of fell apart, and her legs straightened under the covers with such a convulsive kick that Miss Fran, Grandma's old cat, leaped off the bed in a flying arc and landed on the dresser, and then went stamping off as dignifiedly as possible.

"My stockings! Get my stockings," Grandma yelled, heaving out of her dressing gown with a fierce windmill flailing of arms. "We'll see if that wild-eyed Irishman can come bounding back whenever it suits him."

Cathy and Bettina were tugging at the stockings on

the bony old legs. "I don't remember Uncle Pat's eyes being wild," Bettina said. "And, anyway," she went on in a tone of sweet reason, "if Uncle Pat just went away to look after a diamond mine and he comes home with oodles and gobs of diamonds for Faith, won't everything be lovely?"

Grandma didn't seem to hear. She went into the closet, where they could hear her exploding to herself. "Rover! Vagabond! Black-hearted villain!" She came out, giving the draw strings of her petticoat a savage jerk. "Stay around here, you two. I'll have your night things sent over later."

"Grandma, I can't stay here. I've got to go back with you. I've got a friend coming to the house to rehearse a dance." Cathy's voice had jumped to a squeak, but she couldn't control it. It was all wrong to have broken her news like this, her thoughts went limping along, but Grandma hadn't even heard. Grandma never could remember that Cathy was practically an adult and had certainly taken an adult's place at home for years.

Still in her petticoat, Grandma piled her hair high, put on her best feather hat, and speared the whole with a rhinestone hatpin. "Patrick McQueen won't stay long, I can promise you that." She drew herself up to full, majestic height. "The nerve of that man! The miserable sinner!" she muttered to herself in the mirror.

Once more the weight of Cathy's anxiety pushed out her plea in a squeak. "Please don't make us stay here, Grandma! Please!"

"If Uncle Pat isn't going to stay long, we ought to see him," Bettina announced firmly. And then because, when Bettina got worked up, there was no stop, no caution in her, she rushed on outrageously, "We *ought* to see a real miserable sinner, Grandma. Miss Beason, our Sun-

day School teacher, says to know sin when you see it is
the true safeguard against the devil."

Grandma sucked in her old cheeks as though she were
struggling inside somehow. For the first time she really
looked at her granddaughters. "About sin—" she finally
pronounced, "your Miss Beason probably doesn't know
beef from bull's foot. But the principle is sound. Come
along." Impulsively she bent to kiss each girl. Her gaze
rested a long moment on the slender oval of Cathy's face,
on her intensely serious gray-green eyes. An approving
hand touched the cascade of shining, coppery hair and
then rested on the slim shoulders in the pale pink sweater.
Only when her glance traveled over the navy pleated
skirt to the pink ballet slippers did her craggy brows draw
together questioningly.

The fright in Cathy leveled off a little. "I'm breaking
them in for a dance rehearsal," she explained. "I meant
to take them off."

But once again Grandma didn't seem to hear. "You're
nearly seventeen, aren't you, Cathy?"

Cathy nodded. "In two weeks."

"Faith was nineteen when she married Patrick Mc-
Queen. Forewarned is forearmed," Grandma added as
an afterthought. "Perhaps it's well for you to see what
happens to a headstrong heart."

It was a peculiar thing for Grandma, so brisk, so matter
of fact, to say. And somehow to have it applied to Faith
seemed even more out of character. It would have been
easy to imagine Gerry having a headstrong heart. And
then because her own heart was so full of bewildering
new interests, all centering on Rex, she wondered whether
Grandma would consider her headstrong to be planning
a career of ballet when for three years she'd been geared

to giving every waking moment out of school to her brothers and sisters.

Her fingers fumbled as she pushed the little crystal cat's-eyes through the buttonholes down the back of Grandma's best green velvet. That was mystifying, too— why should Grandma want to be so dressy when she plainly had no use for Uncle Pat?

They had to take the long way round to Faith's because Grandma couldn't go over the hill. Grandma stumped along fast, obvious gale velocity building up in her with each step, so that she seemed to forget all about her bad knee and barely touched the ground with her stick.

Among all the overlapping pressures, Cathy's thoughts were on planning how she would ask Cora to help her move the dining table to one side so that she and Rex could have the dining room for their practice space. For, of course, Grandma and Gerry would be in the living room and in and out of the long hallway that she'd counted on earlier in the day before the Paris hat had arrived.

They found Gerry cross-legged on the floor, little piles of sheet music all around the big puffs of her red wool skirt. "I'm hunting up Pat's favorites so they'll be on the piano when he gets here."

Cousin Rick, Gerry's brother, was there, too. "I thought we ought to have a real welcoming committee," Gerry explained.

Rick's eyes, magnified by the thick-lensed glasses he wore, greeted them with his quiet glint of amusement. Grandma's glare sort of chewed its way through him. Humph! it said. Although Rick was her grandson, Grandma invariably acted, as Bettina said, as though he were maybe a cactus cross she was rising above, because he thought so much of horses instead of applying himself to what was considered a marvelous chance for a boy of twenty-one in a bank. And as all the family knew, too, when Rick wasn't thinking about horses, he had his nose in a book storing up all kinds of unrelated facts. A delightful retreat from the everyday world, Rick himself was always the first to admit, but a retreat which, in spite of her own passion for reading, Grandma found extremely irritating. Now he waved a languid greeting over the top of his book.

Cathy saw Grandma wince. She couldn't stand that languid manner of Rick's, either, but that, as Bettina was always quick to point out in his defense, could be due to the fact that being an assistant teller and counting money all day doesn't build muscles.

"Faith's locked herself in and won't talk," Rick said.

"She won't, eh?" Grandma mounted the stairs and began to pound furiously on Faith's door with her stick. "Come out of there, my girl," she called. "You hear me?"

"Anyone could hear her a block away," Bettina whispered to Cathy. It was true. Grandma had great power, considering she seemed to be nothing but bones and blue veins.

Faith refused to open her door. Then Grandma began to roar about pride and family honor and the leopard—meaning Uncle Pat—absolutely never changing his spots even though he might drip charm from every pore. Grandma's speech was punctuated by little snatches of song from Gerry as she found her own favorites among the music. The very fact that Faith, usually so acquiescent, so passive, refused to answer Grandma was quite a surprise.

Rick put his fingers in his ears and gave the girls a conspiratorial wink. There was now a crackle to Grandma's voice like fire licking at cellophane, and a great pounding of her stick made it even more fearsome. Watching the hands on the grandfather's clock in the hall, Cathy felt every nerve in her body willing time to stand still while Grandma wore herself out, so that Rex should not arrive in the middle of a family fracas. If she had known what a scene there was to be, she would never have volunteered to take Grandma the news.

Unable to stand it longer, she grabbed Bettina. "Come on! Help me move the dining table." But even as they opened the door, they heard the clink of silver, and there was Cora moving in ponderous haste and heady excitement around the table, now extended with two extra leaves, and setting each place with the best crystal and china.

"If there was one thing Mr. McQueen liked, it was the best of everything on his table, and it's no more than right and proper that the family gather around in a welcoming meal his first night." Cora drew back admiringly. "Can't be a table in all Africa to match this!"

"But Grandma's not exactly welcoming," Bettina pointed out.

An iridescent goblet in Cora's towel-wielding hands flashed its ruby, sapphire, and gold brilliance into her flushed, excited face. "Your Grandma can roar like a lion and then quick as a wink go all soft butter inside."

"But it's too early to set that table," Cathy pleaded. "I was counting on pushing the table over so a boy who is coming could teach me a dance here."

"There's the living room for dancing, and I'm sure your cousin Rick will be glad to help you roll back the rug."

"But this isn't the kind of dancing you do in front of your whole family," Bettina explained for Cathy. "Why, I bet your niece Bessie didn't practice the high fandango on that elephant with her grandmother and all her cousins and everybody watching!"

Cora's speculative attention was on the edge of the carving knife that she was testing on her thumb. "Well, there's no moving the table now." And then softening at the sight of Cathy's frustrated expression, she added, "Why, bless your heart, I'm sure your boy friend will be glad to come back some other time when you explain."

Something within Cathy recoiled, shocked, that anyone would refer to Rex by such an ordinary term as "boy friend." Her mouth opened in protest, but closed again as she recognized the futility of trying to explain. She stepped back into the hall, moving carefully, so that the bleak hollowness inside wouldn't spread. You didn't just casually tell a person like Rex to come back some other time. You just didn't! It was still too unbelievable that he was coming at all. And he probably wouldn't bother to come back. There were plenty of other girls, better dancers, too, she had to admit honestly, who would just jump at the chance to be his partner.

"There's the den," Bettina suggested softly. "You could use the den, maybe, if it isn't too full of Faith's stuff."

A forlorn hope quickened in Cathy. A hope that proved to be not only forlorn but utterly untenable. At least a dozen cartons of old clothes that Faith had collected for the foreign mission orphans jammed every inch of floor space that wasn't taken up by stacks and stacks of un-wearables waiting to be cut into strips for rugs she was hooking for the church bazaar.

"There's the upstairs hall," Bettina put in.

Cathy shook her head. Grandma, winded, was sitting on a top step, but her whole aspect was a declaration that she intended to have her say when breath permitted.

As Cathy and Bettina looked up the stairs, they heard her mutter, "Mad hat business!"

Gerry said to Rick, "It *is* kind of mad, you know, but dreamy mad—the kind of thing only Pat would do."

It was a relief to Cathy when Bettina drifted off to the kitchen. She turned back into the den, sank into a pile of rug rags like a leggy young bird in a cavernous nest. Her shoulders were shaking, but she wasn't crying, of course. It was going to be bad enough to have to tell Rex when he arrived that he could not come in, without presenting a blotchy face and red eyes. "You're not going to cry! You're not; you're not!" she told herself. She was so preoccupied in her self-enclosed world that she almost jumped when Gerry stood beside her.

"Why, honey, you mustn't take it like this. Grandma didn't mean to frighten you. Every family has rows once in a while. It's just that you've lived alone with your father and the children and Mee Chow so long that you haven't really gotten in on grown-up problems much." She went on confidentially. "Grandma's raising a rumpus just because she hates to have Faith hurt. After all, Pat did walk out on her, and it's been pretty rugged." She paused, patting Cathy's hand. "Pat's charming and brilliant. And yet there's the other side, too, the side that sends him off on adventure with no thought for anyone but himself. But Faith will have to decide what she wants to do."

In a dim way Cathy realized that Gerry was talking to her as an adult, and at any other time she would have responded gratefully. But a lump blocked her throat, and all she could manage was a nod.

As though Gerry sensed this, she said abruptly, "There's something else worrying you, isn't there, darling?"

In a surge, as she leaned on the protective circle of

Gerry's arm, the whole pent-up story of the lost miracle
came tumbling out. "You saw Rex Emory dance last year
when you came to the Christmas party at school. Remember?"

"Of course, I remember. He was wonderful."

"Well, he's graduated since, but he came back to see
the folk-dance festival last week. Somehow or other,
I lost the headdress to my costume. I was supposed to
turn it back to Miss Allison, the gym teacher, and I just
couldn't find it. I'd hunted everywhere but on the stage,
and so after everyone else had gone, I went back there
to look, and Rex was dancing there by himself. He's the
only student who ever had permission to use the stage
after school for his own practice. Of course, our school
never had a dancer like Rex before; Miss Allison says
they're just not born very often." Cathy paused a moment in reverie. "It's still something I can hardly believe
happened—but it did. You see, I was just overwhelmed
watching him. I'd never been close up to a really marvelous dancer before."

As she talked, a far-away raptness came into her eyes.
Cathy was suddenly right back there on the stage, the
forest-scene backdrop used in their folk dance behind her.
Again she felt the prickle of awe, the exhilaration, as
when Rex had risen high in the air in a magnificent
leap, soaring effortlessly, cloud-light, and then landed with
thistledown buoyancy at her feet. While he was still in
the air, something had begun to happen to her own
normal sense of balance, because she had the curious
sensation of being borne upward herself into a new and
rarefied atmosphere.

The sensation continued as Rex stood before her, the
hard muscles rippling under the smooth, dark skin of his
arms crossed over his chest in the white T-shirt, the bril-

liance of his dark eyes registering a surprising recognition.

"Hello," he said. "I remember you. You're one of the
girls who danced this afternoon. I remember you dis-
tinctly. You had a nice lightness and a natural rhythmic
sense."

"I did?" Cathy gasped unprepared. "I didn't know I
was anything special." She paused in confusion and then
wound up lamely, "I mean—my goodness!"

Rex moved to a record player in the wings, put on a
record, and there was the music to her dance. "Would
you dance again for me?"

Paralyzing panic rose in Cathy. Dance for Rex? Oh,
no! She couldn't! She couldn't even *move*.

Rex had started to dance by himself. When he crossed
the stage again to where she stood he took her hand, and
after a preliminary stumble she was dancing, too. Dancing in a way she'd never danced before, a current of
strength, fresh and spontaneous, rushing through her, a
yielding softness that was part of the happiness exploding
in the air.

When that dance was done, Rex had put on another
record, music that Cathy knew but had never danced to,
and without speaking he began to dance again. She
watched, and then when he held out his hand once more,
there was his persuasive charm, a mysterious power, some
magnetism she couldn't begin to understand. Even stilled,
his very being carried glamour and grace; but she had
never, even in a dream, linked herself with this. Then
suddenly she was trying the steps, too.

"Of course I didn't do very well at first," she explained
to Gerry. "But Rex just put the needle back on the record
and had me try again. It was the funniest thing, Gerry.
At first I tried to remember things like how you count

with the phrase and all the names for the steps he was doing, like *pas de chat* and *glissade* and *petit battement* and, oh, everything I'd ever been taught about ballet, and, then, I just forgot it all and yet I knew the steps were coming out of my feet exactly as they should."

"I know what you mean," Gerry told her. "I've had the same thing happen with a paint brush. It's a thrill like nothing else on earth."

"Well, when it was over, Rex said, 'That's it. That's just the feeling I want.' And then he went on talking to me, telling me how he's interested in choreography as well as dancing."

Breath suspended, Cathy relived the incredible scene. "He said he'd been working on an original fairy-tale dance and that he needed a girl with a sort of Snow White quality to dance with him; and he thought that with work maybe I could do it." She broke off in brief self-conscious shyness. "If I take lessons and work, he said."

"But that's wonderful," Gerry cried. "Of course, you can do it." Gerry's enthusiastic response ended in a quick squeeze of pleasure. "This is just the kind of thing you've needed. You were getting to be a little-old-woman-in-a-shoe, or, I should say, a mother hen clucking over the children at home; and that's one reason why I put in a vote for you and Bettina to come here to Faith's for two weeks of complete change instead of going to camp with the others, where you'd just go on clucking."

"But I haven't minded," Cathy broke in.

"I know that," Gerry assured, "and heaven knows you've been busy as a moth in a muff, but if you'll forgive my saying so, your activities have been just about that restricted, too. It strikes me it's time now for, well, for you to blossom out. Matter of fact, Faith should have had a couple of you children over here long ago. It's ridiculous for her to live in this huge place all by herself with a maid to wait on her hand and foot. It's—it's absurd. Actually Faith should have gone with Pat." She shrugged. "But you know how Faith's lived to herself in a remote dream bubble all her life. In any case, you ought to have more time for yourself."

Maybe Gerry's idea was the answer. Cathy's thoughts seized and examined the prospect of Faith's taking a couple of the children for a year. It would certainly give her more time to herself, and if the family was for it, Dad wouldn't mind—maybe. But Pipper was too little, too babyish yet at five, to be trusted to Faith's withdrawn dreaminess; the twins' trigger-edged tempers would floor Faith in a day; and Tess would never get her arithmetic by herself. Of course, there was Cora, but if Uncle Pat stayed home this time the house would be bursting with company, and Cora would be too busy. With a sigh Cathy discarded the whole idea.

Her thoughts returned to the immediate problem she faced. "So you see," she wound up, "Rex will be here any second, and there's just no place for us to practice."

Gerry bounded to her feet, her dark eyes darting around with such determination that they seemed to be daring the walls not to open and create a special new room just right for dance rehearsal. "I've got it! Come on, come on!"

Pulled along, Cathy found herself running through the hall, through the kitchen past an astonished Cora, and, with a pell-mell jangle of Gerry's bracelets and a tap-tap clickety-clack of her high heels, down the basement steps to the big, clean laundry room, where they skidded to a stop in the center. The washing machine moved easily on its casters to the wall, the drying rack was cleared, and Gerry plunked herself down on the bench of the mangle to catch her breath. "Here you are, sweet! It's big and bare and private, and you can bring down that little portable record player Pat used to take on picnics."

Using the edge of the laundry tub as a balancing *barre,* Cathy did a happy *echappé.* Even the soapy smell of the tubs seemed to have taken on the aura of rapturous anticipation. "Oh, you do understand, don't you?"

A sudden whimsical smile lit Gerry's face. "It hasn't been so many years since I was your age, and although, as you know, I loathe getting up early, I was out on a tennis court every morning at six to play with a boy who was my hero that entire summer."

Cathy half turned away. "But this isn't like that at all. I know that I want to be a really good professional dancer. It's strange, though, your using the word 'hero' because that's just what Miss Allison said. I didn't know she'd been watching me dance with Rex, but when we were through, she asked me to come to her office and help pack costumes. She made a little speech about there being a chance for growth in hero worship. It's something like after you've outgrown the worship itself you should have grown."

Gerry nodded understandingly.

"There was something else, too, that I didn't half pay attention to because I was in such a hazy daze," Cathy went on, thinking aloud. "It was about how some people have the personal charm and power to inspire hero worship, and they have the power to hurt, too." A sudden troubled look came into Cathy's face. "Why, that's almost what you were trying to tell me about Uncle Pat, isn't it? And Grandma said, 'Forewarned is forearmed.'" A faint chill of foreboding trickled through the warmth of her happiness.

"But, pet," Gerry got up and gave her black blouse a

brisk smooth down into her red skirt, "in art school we
learned that art of all kinds is fifty per cent skill and fifty
per cent emotion which you must express with your skill.
Perhaps it's the same with ballet. And now this hero worship will help you with the emotion, and the rest—the
skill—is something you'll acquire as you study. Anyway,
remember that Rex is just a nice new friend who has already given you something wonderful—a goal."

The eerie chill evaporated. "Oh, Gerry, you'll never
know—I felt so left out at school. It seemed as though
everyone else was planning what they wanted to do about
college and a career, and I just didn't seem to have any
special talent. I felt that I was such an *in-between-ish*
person. I guess you wouldn't know about that. You've
always been so talented and everything was so easy for
you."

"Easy? What a funny word to use. Sure, I had talent
—my first crayon scribblings had zip and action, and cows
and people looked like cows and people. But talent isn't
everything. Talent didn't make life easy when Dad and
Mother were killed in that smash-up." Her voice broke.
Then she went on huskily. "It wasn't easy living with
Grandma, who wanted me to be a lady when I was born
a tomboy. It wasn't easy to see her push Rick into the
bank because it's a good safe place and she happens to
know the president. Of course, I still think I can wangle
him back to Stanford in the fall and into a line he'll like
better."

"Like horses?" Cathy asked, smiling.

Gerry's clear contralto was even again. "Well, he can't
earn his living with horses—at least not right now. Anyway, from Rick's point of view the word is horse, singular,
not horses. You see," she explained, "his real love is
dressage."

"Dressage?" Cathy questioned. "What's dressage?"

"It's the art of horsemanship. Equitation is another name for it, loosely speaking."

"How can you call it art?"

"Get Rick to tell you," Gerry suggested. "You'll see it really does come under that heading." She paused thoughtfully. "Actually it's a kind of subtle language developed between rider and horse, so that, eventually, after ages of patient training, the horse responds almost to your thoughts, to an absolutely uncanny minimum of direction, at any rate. And that's when you can enter the big horse shows."

The words practically popped out with Cathy's astonishment. "Rick ride in a horse show? Why, he's so—so droopy and limp!"

"Not when he's on a horse. Something wonderful happens to his spine then. Something like what happened to you when you danced with Rex, I imagine." Gerry's full-hearted exuberance sparkled. "Not that I'm literally lumping Rex and Rick's dream horse together, you understand!"

Cathy shook her head. "I don't know where I've been, not to know about Rick's dream horse. I thought it was just horses in general he was crazy about. It's kind of startling to discover a person's secret dreams, isn't it?" Beneath the familiar outlines of Rick's lanky, seemingly lazy figure a new personage emerged. It was strange to see him so revealed, just as she herself was emerging into newness, too, in the first steps of the realization of her own secret dream.

"Matter of fact, it was Pat who fired Rick's dream," Gerry told her. "He used to take Rick along to the horse shows. If I remember rightly, he even talked about getting him a horse sometime."

"Uncle Pat took me to my first ballet, too," Cathy breathed in remembrance. "The first and only professional ballet I've ever seen," she amended. Now all that would change. She'd save every penny of her allowance so that she could see as many as possible during the season. In the momentary silence the drip of a laundry faucet marked her heartbeats. Then it was going thumpety-thump—two beats to every drip. The listening tautness in her face was mirrored in Gerry's expression. "Isn't that the doorbell?"

"Oh, it might be Pat," Gerry squealed.

Cathy's unsteady hand flew to adjust the ribbon that held back her hair. "It might be Rex!"

3

Footprints in the Shrubbery

THE WHOLE FAMILY with the exception of Faith was gathered in the hall as Cora opened the door. Even Jimbo seemed infected with their tense expectancy; long ears drooped over the sad dignity of his cocker nose poked between the stair rails to watch proceedings in the hall below.

"It's Cathy's Walt," Cora announced.

Cathy's embarrassment at Cora's blunt use of the possessive was lost in her sharp anxiety. Bettina had said Walt was due to come *after* dinner, and now here he was ahead of time. Walt was not a boy you could hurry in and out. A decided mind of his own was expressed in every characterizing motion of his tall, solid figure, in his square, determined chin, somehow even in the cocky crest of cream-colored hair.

"This is my day off. Dad and I went fishing and I thought maybe you could use a striped bass." He made

36

a motion to hand Cathy a huge paper-wrapped bundle.

Rick said, "Hey, no sportsman's fish should ever go to the kitchen without being first admired."

Cathy almost groaned as Walt all too eagerly un-wrapped his prize and held it up by the tail for inspection. The last bit of daylight coming through the window brought out the brassy reflections along its olive-green back, but Cathy could not bring forth her usual enthusiasm as she strained her ears for other footsteps on the porch.

"A beaut," Rick pronounced over the gusts of admiration from Bettina and Gerry.

"Sixteen pounds four ounces," Walt announced proudly. "Never had such a day; got our limit catch the first two hours we were out."

Rick's lanky figure drooped against the side window by the door so that Cathy could not see past him.

Rick asked, "What kind of bait did you use?"

"Oh, no!" Cathy thought, with fidgety impatience. "Don't get him started on that!"

"Salt anchovies." Walt laid the bass down on the paper again and wiped his hands on the tail of his blue-checked shirt. "They're your best bet for almost any kind of fish in the bay here."

Cathy swallowed hard, crowding down her longing to ease Walt out while a rush of remembrance brought pictures of Walt teaching her how to back out of the garage; Walt lurching to bat her wild southpaw pitches that always put her to shame in the neighborhood sand-lot games; his easy-going tolerance of the way the little kids always tagged along everywhere they went; and that lace-edged bunch of forget-me-nots with Walt's scribble, "Save me the first six tonight at the Hallowe'en hoe-down." With this kaleidoscope of happy scenes came

something like a stab of disloyalty, as though in her preoccupation with thoughts of Rex there was an obscure
betrayal of their friendship.

She picked up the big bass and was starting for the
kitchen when Walt stopped her with, "Tell Cora Mom's
latest trick is to put an onion, a bay leaf, and a chunk of
carrot inside the fish, wrap it in aluminum foil, and stick
it in the oven." As the swinging door to the kitchen closed
behind her, Cathy heard Walt ask, "Say, am I breaking
in on a family gathering or something?"

When she returned, the family had moved back into
the living room, and it was obvious that someone had told
him about Uncle Pat's imminent arrival because Walt was
saying, "You know, your Uncle Pat's the very person I
ought to see." His direct blue eyes had that far-seeing
look, that special eager glow, that came when he was talking about his inventions. Now he'd whip out a new dia-
gram of wheels, wires, levers, magnetic coils. . . . Instead,
Walt went on, "As I remember, your uncle was Mr. Midas
himself. He could keep ten fingers in ten different pies
and parlay them all into money makers." Walt wiggled
his fingers in ten figurative pies, and Cathy saw the long
scar on the little finger, which was a memento of one of
his inventions.

Bettina began to jump up and down, her eyes enormous
with excitement. "I've just thought of something. If
Uncle Pat's fingers have been in a diamond mine for two
whole years, maybe he'll bring us each a lovely little sack
of diamonds."

"I can't think of a lovelier idea," Gerry said.

Rick wriggled down in his chair. "It doesn't have to be
too much on the small side, either."

"A friend of mine's father sent her a little sack of salt
tied on a post card from Salt Lake City," Bettina rushed

on, "but I guess no one at school ever had their very own sack of diamonds fresh from their very own uncle's mine."

Gerry sat down at the piano and played a one finger tune. "If that happens," she chanted, "I'll take one of my very own lovely fresh little diamonds and have it set in my very front tooth."

"Please," Grandma exploded irritably, turning from the desk where she had been writing with a very scratchy pen, "I'm trying to concentrate."

Rick said, "A maharajah in India has a set of diamond eyebrows. They hook over his ears like spectacles. If we each get a whole bag we might go in for something equally spectacular."

Enchanted, Bettina added, "I might give all my friends diamond-studded skate keys for Christmas."

"Anyway, you're right about Pat being a natural for luck in business," Rick said to Walt. "I take it you need some advice in marketing your latest brain child."

"It's just a case of getting the right promotion," Walt's enthusiasm welled out in a gusty grin of delight. "With the proper pitch this little idea should put me through college and keep me going until I get patents on two or three other things I've got almost finished. Now take my new carburetor—"

"I've got all that information you asked me to look up," Bettina interrupted importantly. "I've even—"

Grandma, who all too obviously didn't want to hear details of the new carburetor, sliced off Bettina's words with a jab of her pen. "Didn't you say something about Walt coming to dance with you, Cathy?"

Cathy could feel the question in Walt's startled glance, and the jumbled words in her throat backed down into self-consciousness as Bettina explained, "Oh, Grandma, it isn't Walt who's going to teach Cathy. My gosh, can you imagine Walt doing ballet!" Her snickers developed into side-holding giggles. Only crossing her feet seemed to hold her upright in her mirth.

"I don't know," Gerry protested tactfully from the piano, where she flicked at a grace note. "Walt might bring a new and delightfully rugged touch to the ballet."

Walt shifted his large feet on the rug. "What's all this?" he asked.

"Cathy's going to make ballet a real career," Bettina informed.

After all, Walt had to know sometime. And now it was out, as plain for all to see as a shoe button in the sugar bowl, to use one of Cora's homespun expressions. Walt would just have to get used to the idea that she had a career of her own to plan and work on, but his stunned expression said clearly the idea was going to take time to digest. "Kind of sudden, isn't it? I mean—I always just thought of you being next door unscrambling the twins and stuff like that."

"But the twins are growing up," Cathy faltered.

"And so is Cathy," Gerry added.

Gerry's reassuring smile helped, but Cathy somehow had that guilty feeling tied up with her thoughts of Rex. Once again there was that disturbing stab of disloyalty.

The silence was broken by Rick, who said teasingly, "I was reading the other day about an Indian tribe that puts on a right snappy turtle dance. Now there's something that might be worth watching." His expression questioned Walt, but Walt's eyes were on Bettina, now on all fours doing her own quick version of a turtle dance, her neck popping in and out of her striped shirt, her back a humped shell, all to the accompaniment of turtle talk.

How awful for Rex to come now, Cathy thought. Her nervous glance at the clock told her that Rex was already late. And because the ecstatic anticipation of his arrival had bogged down in a jumble of confusion, exhaustion, and misplaced guilt, she had a longing to grab Bettina and shake the mischief out of her; but just then Gerry's hand darted out and gave Bettina's blue-jeaned seat a playful little paddle. "As a turtle dancer you're a much better pretzel, my lamb."

Rick went on, "Or take the ancient Greeks. One of their favorite stunts was to dance on greased skins to display a nice sense of balance."

Inspired by this to display her own sense of balance, Bettina wound up with a hand stand.

Walt's direct blue gaze lifted to Cathy, and he said abruptly, "Well, I have to get along and clean the rest of my fish. But I'll be back later and tell you about my new idea. I was telling Betts about it yesterday."

As their eyes met, the whole purpose of the day seemed to waver. Walt stood for sixteen years of close friendship. In all those years she couldn't remember a time when she hadn't been glad to see him. How could all that now be changed—changed by a single hour on a stage with a strange boy? She shivered and tried to shrug the confusion away as she followed Walt to the door.

Walt was saying, "I'll make it back about eight?"

If Rex was going to be very late she didn't want Walt coming back at all. "I've never given him the brush-off in my whole life," she thought. But something about Walt's big blond head outlined against the gold and crimson sunset in the open doorway made it hard to answer, so that, even as she struggled for an excuse, the very opposite popped out. "All right," she heard herself say.

Almost as if she knew Cathy needed support, Gerry was right there with a whispered, "Don't look so woebegone, darling. Your Rex will be here any minute now."

"But he's late. He said he'd be here on his way home from his job, where he's teaching an afternoon dancing class. He said it would be about five."

"Oh, well, *about* five can mean anything," Gerry assured.

"I feel so sort of hollow," Cathy confided.

"Maybe what you need is food—a little stuffing for those dancing legs. And speaking of food—" She waved a hand at Cora coming through the kitchen door with a tray on which was the moss rose teapot and a couple of her citron buns.

"I'm taking this upstairs, ma'am," she said to Grandma. "I figured Mrs. McQueen needs a bit of nourishment to help her through the waiting."

"You see, Cora has the right idea," Gerry said to Cathy. "Food, food, beautiful food is what you need, too. You know," she said, including Rick and the others, "I've been thinking—could be nicer for Faith and Pat to have their dinner just by themselves."

Cora came clumping down stairs with the tray. "She won't open her door, ma'am."

"We'll come out and have our dinner now," Gerry told her, "and then we'll stay just long enough to give Pat a big welcome."

"He'll get no welcome from me," Grandma announced. "I'm not even trusting my memory for all the things I have to say. It'll be written down." And she jabbed at the paper with her pen.

Gerry and Rick exchanged a raised eyebrow look as Grandma went on, "If that rogue thinks he can just sail in here after two years—"

"Oh, I wonder what Faith will do," Gerry wanted to know. "Two years is a long time."

Rick said, "Well, such things have happened. Take that old Greek hero, Ulysses. He was something like seven years on his way. Of course, he claimed it was unfavorable winds that drove him off his course and forced him to dally with the lotus-eaters."

Cathy's thoughts raced with the click of her knitting needles that were adding rows to a red sock for Pipper. What were the real, the true, unfavorable winds that had kept Uncle Pat?

Rick said, "One thing you'll have to say for Pat, he left Faith holding a nice hunk of cabbage."

Grandma gave a disapproving sniff at Rick's inelegant choice of words. Bettina's head lolled back on her neck. "Don't you wish a window would suddenly open in the ceiling so we could look up and see what Faith is doing?" she sighed. "I wish we could see if she's trying on her hat. It must be awful to get a beautiful Paris hat when you're too old to enjoy it."

Gerry laughed. "Old!"

"Well, how old is she?" Bettina asked.

"Five years older than my left foot," Rick told her. And that was easy because they all knew Rick was twenty-one.

"It *would* be interesting to know what Faith is doing," Gerry agreed.

"Utterly ridiculous, keeping herself locked up," Grandma muttered.

Most of Cathy's thoughts had been following her own problem of Rex versus Walt, but, as she glanced up from her knitting, the twinkle that came through the lazy slit of Rick's half-closed eyes brought her back to the family conversation.

"If you ladies are so consumed by curiosity, the easy way to satisfy it is for our agile young turtle dancer here to weasel around on the balcony from the guest room to Faith's room and peek in through the French doors."

A disapproving sigh came out of Grandma, but if she had any intention of forbidding the plot, it was too late, for Bettina was off like a flash.

Gerry echoed Grandma's disapproval of Rick's brash suggestion; then she jumped up on the sofa to look at herself in the full-length mirror. She turned quickly to observe the swirl of her skirt and pulled a black curl out over her ear, letting it snap back. "Oh, I wish Pat would come! I wish we knew what Faith will do! The suspense is killing me."

"I wish Rex would come—I wish he would come this very minute, so that we could rehearse our dance alone before Walt comes back," Cathy's thoughts repeated while once again her ears strained at each snapping twig outdoors, each drift of sound that might be a footstep. "It's such an on-your-mark-get-set feeling with no one yelling *go*," she said to Gerry.

"Geraldine," Grandma's voice thundered, "get down from that sofa. When I was young, we acted like ladies."

Gerry sat down with a plunk and twiddled her thumbs in mock gravity. "I *am* a lady," she said demurely. "If you don't believe it, just look in my top drawer and you'll see three and a half pairs of the purest white gloves a lady ever—why, what's the matter, sweet?"

Bettina's small hand groped for the banister, her small pixie face under its slash of black bang had a pinched, scared look.

"What is it, Betts? What happened?" Cathy demanded. What could she have seen in Faith's room? The thought was there in every face, in the barrage of questions.

"Nothing," Bettina blurted. "Nothing—really—I just got dizzy on the balcony, I guess."

"You, dizzy!" Cathy scoffed. "You, the champion banana eater while you stand on your head?"

"Something scared me." Bettina's voice did register fright. To Cathy's ears it also registered the unsteadiness of falsehood. Usually, when Bettina sounded like this, Cathy could almost fill in the details of whatever small crime her sister had committed, but now she was stumped.

"A seagull flapping by?" Rick suggested.

"Yes, that was it—a flappy old seagull."

While the others smiled at the childish way Bettina snatched at Rick's seagull, Cathy's suspicion that Bettina wasn't telling the truth became a certainty.

Bettina walked over to the big bear rug that stretched under the piano and lay down, burying her face in the fur. Cathy put aside her knitting and went to sit beside her. "Now, Betts, there's something you're not telling, isn't there?"

"At least you could tell us what Faith was doing," Grandma demanded, with strained patience.

"I didn't see her," Bettina mumbled through the fur. "She wasn't in her room."

"What?" The whole family rocked back on their heels; that is, all but Rick, who said sensibly, "She could have been in her closet or in the bathroom."

But Cathy knew there was something else, something frightening, that Bettina was deliberately trying to hide. She could feel little tremors of fear pass along Bettina's firm, slim sides as she squished deeper into the rug, her face still hidden. Suddenly, the bright, beckoning world of Rex and the ballet slipped away, and Cathy was once again what Gerry had referred to as her little-old-woman-in-the-shoe self, all motherly concern for Betts. And pretty soon she saw with relief that Bettina's arm crooked forward to feel the cold kiss of the bear's nose in her hand, and she knew that Betts was pretending she was part bear herself, a game all the children had played with this rug. For a moment Cathy wished she could play it again, too, and shuck off all the complications of the grown-up world about her.

Rick had touched a match to the wood laid in the fireplace, for San Francisco evenings are chilly even in summer, and now every rosy shaft of firelight rested on gleaming, polished wood, on the deep reds of Bokhara rugs and the pale green and gray upholstery. There was Faith's harp in its green cover, a harp whose sweet, rippling arpeggios hadn't been heard for two years. The books in their ceiling-high, recessed shelves had a special glossy red-and-goldness, all so different from home, where a house spilling over with children gave everything a tag-end, much-handled appearance. A queer disenchantment crept over her. This lovely room should hold only happiness and contentment. But even Gerry's air of gay festiveness, even the crackly coziness of the fire couldn't thaw out that wind-battered look of fierce defiance that Grandma had. Poor Grandma!

Now, as Cathy watched, Bettina's head shifted a little— she knew the old pretending hadn't worked. She was still shaken, scared. What could it be? Cathy bent down and whispered, "Come on, Betts, we'll go into the den where we can talk." But Bettina closed her eyes; her whole face seemed closed, too.

Rick said, "Come on, sprouts, let's eat." And at that Bettina jumped up and dashed into the kitchen as though, Cathy thought, glad for any diversion that would turn attention away from her.

Gerry tried to pry Grandma away from her writing at the desk, but Grandma said, "Not for me. I couldn't eat a mouthful."

In the kitchen Rick went over to the stove, lifted the cover on a pot, and inhaled deeply. "Wouldn't it be cozy to gather round the board right here and save all that elegance in the dining room for the lord and lady of the manor?"

"Yes, let's," Bettina urged. And then she asked, "Why are you crying, Cora?"

Rick said, "It's that onion on her chest." There really was a little green onion on Cora's bosom with just a nibble out where she had snatched a bite and then dropped it in a hurry, as she was always doing.

Suddenly there was Cora hiccoughing through her sniffles and saying, "Do you remember me when Mr. Mc-Queen was here?"

"Of course," Gerry said. And Rick added gallantly, "You're the same fine figure of a woman."

Then Cora sat down; the chair under her shuddered and creaked. "No, I'm not, sir," she choked. "It was after Mr. McQueen left the last time that it started. I couldn't get used to the quiet and the loneliness, and Mrs. Mc-Queen just walked through the house like a shadow, and to fill in my time I took to piecing and snacking; and before I knew it, I'd eaten myself fat, sir, and whatever Mr. McQueen is going to say I don't know."

Cathy found herself patting Cora's heaving hump of shoulder, while Gerry poured her a glass of water.

"If I don't watch out, I'll be like my niece Rosetta who got nicknamed Rose-eater with a waist line of forty-eight inches just because she can't let hot cakes and maple syrup alone. Matter of fact I've been thinking lately I ought to leave here and give Rosetta a hand. She's too heavy for housework, and that's a fact."

"Oh, no." Bettina and Cathy started the proper chorus, knowing full well that nothing could drag Cora away from

Faith, but knowing, too, that she loved to be begged to stay, that it was really a game. "You can't leave, Cora. Promise you won't leave!"

"Of course, you can't leave," Gerry said, "especially not with Pat coming home. When I think of the parties they used to have and the heavenly goodies you used to make for them, Cora—"

This was just the cheer Cora needed. "I'm going to change," she vowed. "When Mr. McQueen's home, I'll be busier, and I won't eat all the time. I'll get my shape back. You'll see if I don't." She got up and began piling banana fritters into a silver serving dish in her old efficient way.

Rick speared the ham with its pineapple glaze onto a platter and started to slice it, while Cathy wrapped one of Cora's colossal aprons twice around herself and began to toss the salad.

"Heavy on the garlic there," Rick ordered.

"Ugh!" Gerry grunted. "We don't want to be breathing garlic into our handsome, dashing uncle's face when we see him for the first time in two years."

Cathy paused, a forkful of curly, crisp endive suspended in midair. "I wonder if the parties will be like the ones they used to have?" Oh, surely Uncle Pat and Faith would consider it an honor to include Rex's name on the invitation list!

Bettina asked, "Did you come to the parties here?"

Rick nodded ruefully. "If I'd had the sense of a half-baked oyster, I'd have buttonholed Pat right then. Of course, I may even yet realize my fond hope." Cathy now knew, anything Rick labeled "fond hope" in that eager way of course had to do with his dream horse. "You young ladies may or may not be aware of the fact that all you need in life is one good horse—one good horse and you're sitting on velvet."

Everyone took a place at the kitchen table, and Bettina said, "That sounds nice."

Rick went on, "At the time your Uncle Pat—er—disappeared, we had a little deal on whereby he was to stake me to a certain filly. That was a horse of high courage who fulfilled every sweet promise of her youth. Had I been her owner I would today be a happy man—even able to tolerate that gruesome cage where I count other people's money and jot down figures in grubby little books."

"Oh, Mr. Richard," Cora exclaimed, astonished, "you look so fine and gentlemanly there in the bank. Whoever wouldn't think you were having a fine time?"

Rick frowned at the yam on his plate. "That's the point, Cora. No one would, or does, or did; no one but Pat. Of course, it's still possible I can interest him in an investment in my behalf." There was the timbre of excitement in his voice, and his knife cut through a pickled fig balanced on a banana fritter.

"Don't get your horsey hopes up too high," warned Gerry affectionately. "Who knows what's going to happen around here?"

"The way I figure it," Cora put in, "Mr. McQueen must have seen most of all creation by this time and be ready to settle down."

Cathy's mind took inventory of her family. It seemed especially important that Uncle Pat come home to stay this time. Everyone needed him. All hearts would rush out in welcome—maybe even Grandma's, in spite of her fury. Wasn't there something that had prompted her to wear her very best dress for the homecoming? Yet how could Faith forget those two years when Uncle Pat was an adventurer? She was increasingly aware of the sensation of darting between two worlds—her own and Faith's, aware of the similarity between them, the awful waiting. Unable to wait now for the meal to come to an end, the talk to wind up, she excused herself and went swiftly back through the house to the front door. Once more her eyes peered through the dark cavern of the night, straining. It was terribly late, but still— As she stood there, the very cadence of the letters R-E-X spelled their kingly meaning in her thoughts. Well named, it sang, king of ballet. *Premier danseur.* You couldn't turn off such a song. Not all at once. But the ugly truth was crushing in on her, piercing the soft rosiness of her dreams. He wasn't coming. He'd forgotten all about their date. The certainty bounced in her glazed mind, which refused to accept it.

The soft, scrambling sound of Jimbo shifting position in the upstairs hall turned her unhappy thoughts in that direction. She was glad to look up, to try to forget the basement laundry room so excitingly prepared, with the little record player on the mangle bench. A new kinship with Faith, a longing to comfort and be comforted sent her racing upstairs. Jimbo's thudding tail welcomed her. Stretching happily, he got to his feet, thrust a moist nose into her hand. She hesitated in front of Faith's closed door, her bruised mind going over the incidents of the late afternoon and evening. One by one the other members of the family had knocked at this door and been turned down. She moved down the hall to an open window, glad for the bracing rush of cool air in her face. Looking out she saw a long-past-bedtime flight of black phoebes swoop through the small, milky radiance of the nearby street light. Involuntarily her eyes tried to penetrate further the swirling fog, but even the circle of cypress along the driveway, with its curious list from years of wind off the Pacific, was indistinct—and no man's figure approached.

Without warning, bewildered hurt turned into baffled fury, surging anger that included all men. How dare Uncle Pat treat Faith like this! How dare he keep her on tenterhooks, waiting—waiting—waiting, until it suited his convenience to turn up! Did he think his irresistible charm would smooth over the heartache? The embarrassment? She moistened her dry lips. Rex's own charm was of the same brand.

Her ear, attuned to her thoughts, picked up a faint but unmistakable sneeze from the outside. Instantly alert, nerves trembling, she peered out the window again. "Who's there?" she called out. She was sure there had been a sound. Positive. Certain. But there was no answer—only the night wind; no figure so far as she could tell in the darkness.

She turned back to the hall to find Gerry just coming up the stairs, her whole expression one of comforting solicitude. "You mustn't mind, pet. Rex forgot, I guess, but he'll probably think of your date later and phone."

"I could phone him." The words leaped out in a jet of hope.

Gerry's head shook gently. "I wouldn't. I'd let him do the phoning." Gerry's merry face was sober. "No matter what happens, remember your ambition to become a ballet dancer doesn't depend on this date or on Rex."

But Cathy knew her whole dream of becoming a great dancer was wrapped around Rex. The endless hours of practice, the discipline, the struggle ahead would all be channeled to the ultimate goal of making herself worthy of being Rex's partner. In spite of Gerry's wise counsel, the temptation to phone Rex was so great that every muscle seemed to stretch with an unbearable sense of urgency to that black instrument there in the hall below. And then, surprisingly, shatteringly, the phone rang, and Cathy's ballet-slippered feet were wings as she skimmed down the stairs.

As her tremulous hello came out, Bettina and Rick burst in from the kitchen. Grandma jolted wide awake, her old face twitching with questioning eagerness. Cora stood at the kitchen door.

"Is it Uncle Pat?" Bettina demanded. "Is it?"

Numbly Cathy reported, "It's Mrs. Brownlee, the lady next door." Then turning back to the phone, she listened to the utterly astonishing message. "I'll tell my aunt," Cathy said. "Yes. Yes. We'll look into it. Thank you very much." She hung up. "Mrs. Brownlee says there's been a man hanging around the house here. She saw him a while ago and then got so worried about it she thought she ought to call." After the disappointing shock of finding that it wasn't Rex calling, Mrs. Brownlee's message had been just a blur of words to be mechanically repeated; but the reaction of the family now brought Cathy to a realization of their mystifying importance. "Why, that explains the sneeze I heard outside a little while ago," she said.

"What in the world—" Grandma started among the hubbub of exclamations.

"It couldn't be Uncle Pat. He'd come right in." This was Gerry speaking.

"I'll go take a look," Rick said.

"I'll get you the flashlight." Cora moved in ponderous haste to the desk drawer.

From the window they watched the circle of light in Rick's hand, and then it disappeared as he moved away from their field of vision. The anxious concern in Gerry's face took on further soberness. "What if he does find a burglar or intruder—he's only armed with a flashlight."

Once again Cora moved in ponderous speed to the closet. "I could at least give him the fire extinguisher."

"Fire extinguisher?" Grandma questioned, with a testy snort.

"It proved mighty handy for my nephew Delbert," Cora started, her voice coming out in puffing gusts. "Got caught on his own back porch with a rattlesnake—grabbed the fire extinguisher—sprayed the snake with carbon monoxide—"

"Dioxide," Gerry breathed in correction.

"Froze it stiffer than a brick of ice cream and then took his time about carrying it away. So if it could freeze a snake, it could freeze a burglar, I guess," she wound up in triumph.

Cathy saw Grandma and Gerry exchange glances, further impatience from Grandma, and amused indulgence from Gerry. Maybe they'd read the same newspaper story about the snake last week. Of course, it could have been about Cora's nephew. And then she forgot all about this speculation as Rick came in the front door.

"Well, there's no one out there now, but there has been, because there are a man's footprints in the earth behind the rhododendrons."

"And I definitely heard someone sneeze out there," Cathy supplemented tensely.

But who could it have been and what was he doing, everyone wondered. The puzzlement was broken by a jerking breath from Bettina. "I know," she choked. "I saw him." For a second her glance was averted, and then, eyes wide, she plunged on as though in a torrent of unburdening. "That's what scared me out on the balcony. Faith wasn't in her room, but this fierce old ugly man was on the balcony with a little white envelope in his hand, and when he saw me he crawled over the railing real fast and went down the jasmine trellis."

Gerry broke the stunned silence by repeating, "Old?"

"Well, pretty old—and fierce—and ugly-looking. Kind of like a pirate with a beard." Bettina's gaze fastened on her blue-jeaned legs, and her stumbling inadequacy, which might have been improvisation, gave Cathy the impression once again that she was holding something back. But Cathy put her arm around her sister's small, shaking shoulders as Grandma's cane stabbed the floor.

Grandma pushed herself to her feet with a mighty effort. "Faith!" she bellowed.

To their further surprise, Rick took command. "I'll talk to her." And oddly enough, when Rick knocked at her door, Faith appeared.

Looking into the upstairs hall, Cathy could see the strain in Faith's pale face. The filmy white robe with its anenome print defined her tall slenderness. There was strain in the huskiness of her voice, too, and it showed in the way her fingers clasped and unclasped nervously while Rick explained about the telephone call, the finding of the footprints behind the rhododendrons, and Bettina's story.

"But I didn't hear anything," Faith insisted. "Of course, I was out of my room while I took a long, hot bath."

Rick scratched his head. "Beats me. You didn't give anyone a little white envelope?"

"Of course, I didn't." Her voice was taut with vehemence. "I tell you I didn't even hear anyone."

"We'll take a look around your room to see if there's anything upset." Rick's voice trailed off as he went about his search, and then he reappeared in the hall. "Not a thing touched that I can see. If there was someone in there—whatever were you doing, sir?" This last was addressed to Jimbo, who answered by holding up a black cocker paw for shaking. "Fine watch dog, you!"

"Maybe we should call the police," Cora suggested, juggling the fire extinguisher, which she still held.

"Maybe we should," Gerry was willing to concede.

Suddenly Faith flung out both hands. "What would anyone want on my balcony?"

Grandma said apprehensively, "Let's hold our horses. The police might mean unpleasant publicity."

"Yeah, if the police got here just when Pat arrived, it could be doggoned awkward. Too many explanations going on at once."

Rick's words made Faith bite her lip. She was silent a moment, and then she begged, "Please, let's wait about the police. Pat can call them later if he thinks it best."

Was it adoration or anger that made Faith's voice tremble as she pronounced Pat's name? Cathy wondered. She tried to read the answer in Faith's face, but Faith turned back to her room, and the door closed again. Maybe it's a little of both, Cathy decided. She knew it was possible because that was just what the hollow, fluttery bewilderment inside her said about Rex.

4

Mystery of the Blue Marshmallow Box

IT WAS ALMOST half past eight when Walt came back. His huge, young, solid strength, his brash, boyish cockiness brought welcome relief after the tense strain of waiting, the endless, answerless questioning of mystery piled on mystery.

To her amazement, Cathy was thoroughly glad to see him. A little later, she told herself, she could really face the disappointment and the pain of Rex's nonappearance. But for the time being she pushed them away, something much easier to do with Walt there and her hand diving down in her knitting bag as usual for Pipper's half-finished, small red sock. The comforting click of her needles and the warmth of the fire helped, too.

It also helped to see that Bettina's usual bounce had returned, as though the disclosure of her adventure on the balcony had relieved her of a strange anxiety. (It wasn't until later that Cathy was to wonder why Bettina had been so secretive at first about telling her story.) As the family greeted Walt, Bettina brought out a stack of Cora's cookbooks, with paper markers stuck among the pages, and her high spirits bubbled over as she thrust the armload at Walt. "There's every single almond recipe marked."

"Almond recipes?" Gerry questioned in astonishment. "What's this?"

"I thought it was a new carburetor," Cathy added, feeling that the surprises of the day had achieved an anticlimax with this curious idea of Walt's interest in almond recipes.

"Sure it's a carburetor," Walt agreed. "I'm on the edge of something big there if I just get a bug worked out, but—" He studied his long legs in their clean cords, stretched to the heat of the leaping flames as Rick threw another log on the fire. "Patents and promotion take money, and in the meantime there's college, and that takes money, too—more than I can possibly make in a summer job; and I just got to figuring the other day at breakfast. I mean there's a fast fortune to be made with just an idea—"

"Take the guy who simply bent a little piece of wire and made the bobby pin," Bettina interposed.

"Of course, I can get a scholarship, but I'll still need cash and I've got to help the folks a bit. Dad's not well enough to work full time." Walt paused and ran a hand through his crew cut, while Cathy thought of his mother's good-natured mismanagement. Walt had been helping his folks for several years and would probably always have to.

"Haven't you got a summer job?" Gerry asked.

"Sure. I'm nursemaid to a bunch of horses down at a Burlingame riding academy."

At the word horses Rick's interest kindled. But as though sensing the possibility of a conversational side-track, Bettina demanded, "Tell them about the prunes, Walt."

There was no hurrying Walt. He'd set his own gait, as Cathy knew, and the world could wait. An individualist! Looking at him, Cathy felt the familiar tug of admiration. Actually there was something wonderfully visionary about him. In a way it almost compared with the ripple of vibrancy that was part of Rex when he danced. Only, with Rex it had seemed something poetic, while the motivating force behind the vision in Walt was always earthy.

"Well, there it was," Walt was saying, "right in front of my nose in my breakfast prune dish. Something out of nothing. Something out of nothing had been running through my head. You know, like whoever found that cattail fluff was the business for stuffing life preservers."

"Is it really?" Gerry asked with a glint of laughter.

"Sure. It's still used," Walt said. "Matter of fact, that isn't the whole story of the lowly cattail. There's an entire research center at Syracuse University devoted to cattails, with about eleven hundred uses already cata-logued, not the least of which, I believe, is cattail cookies made from cattail-root flour."

Gerry shook her head at him, amusement mingled with incredulity. "Where do you get hold of such informa-tion?"

"Now go on about the prune pits," Bettina urged Walt.

"So I looked down," Walt resumed, "and there was this prune pit split open, and I just happened to scrape out the center kernel and eat it, and you know what?"

"What?" everyone chorused obligingly.

"Well, it tasted just like an almond. Almost."

"So, don't you see," Bettina skimmed in importantly, "there are simply carloads of prune pits being thrown away every day, and if you take the kernels out and sell them for almonds, you've got something yummy for nothing."

Grandma's old lips twitched skeptically. "And how do you propose to collect the prune pits America discards?"

Walt's amiable, easy grin conceded a certain ridiculousness in this project. "I'd have to get my pits from the big canneries that bottle prune juice."

"And strained baby prunes," Bettina added, "and candy stores that stuff prunes. They've probably got mountains of them just moldering away because no one but Walt has the sense to use them."

"Do they really taste like almonds?" The beginning of real interest sparkled in Gerry's face. "And won't it be a job to get the kernels out of the pits?"

"Any commercial nut cracker will do it," Walt told them.

"And now all we have to do is get some cooked up in exciting recipes," Bettina rushed on, "because people won't be interested in just plain old prune kernels."

"I figured that any recipe that uses almonds would do," Walt said, "just so I have some samples of something really tasty."

Bettina dove into the recipe books and began reading sing-song, "Almond Bavarian cream, almond butter, almond macaroons, almond mocha pie, almond and quince conserve. . . ."

"What do you think, Rick?" Walt's earnest appeal pulled everyone into his warm enthusiasm.

The lazy slit of Rick's eyes closed a minute behind his thick-lensed glasses and then opened to reveal a humorous twinkle. "Well, you just might have quite a keg of pickles there, as they say, if you can put it over."

"You've got to have a really glamorous name, for one thing," Gerry advised, "and a pack of whoopla advertising."

Cathy had been silent through all this, her role of sympathetic listener to Walt's ideas long established. Now even Bettina was mouse-still while Gerry considered. After all, Gerry was in the advertising business; she was right in the center of this kind of thing all day long.

Gerry stood up, finger-tapping her lower lip. Then slowly she began to twirl as though she might start her brain revolving, too, by this bit of action. She looked light and gipsy-free in her rippling red wool skirt. It was like Gerry, Cathy mused, to give herself completely, abandonedly, to anything she did.

Only that very pirouette of lithe, light freeness conjured up a vision of dancing, reminding her of Rex. Like trick photography, the picture of Rex was superimposed on the picture of Gerry—Rex dancing, twirling light and free. And there she was once more caught in that enchanted hour on the school stage.

As from another world Cathy heard Gerry's voice say, "Prumonds—from *prunes* and *almonds.*" She deliberated again. "And your package should have crossed branches of almonds and plum blossoms."

Suddenly Cathy couldn't control the bitter disappointment of the evening. Welling up, it seemed to wrench her heart out of shape all over again. How could Rex have forgotten their date when he'd seemed so intent on seeing her?

Through the hurting haze she came back to the talk in the room. "Of course, of course. That's perfect." The general acclaim subsided as Walt exclaimed with a rueful quirk, "Only trouble is Mom's declared our kitchen out of bounds. I tried to make some burnt almond—pardon me, *prumond*—toffee, and all I succeeded in doing was burning Mom's big skillet and smoking up the curtains. Frankly, she takes a pretty dim view of the whole subject."

"Cora will let us experiment here." Bettina's enthusiasm was as contagious as Walt's. "I'll bet she'd have some good ideas, too. Why, she even knows how to cook whale flipper. A nephew sent her some from Alaska."

Gerry's expression registered fascinated merriment. "Cora's nephews certainly get around, not to mention her nieces."

"We ought to try talking about a tennis match in Tibet," Rick suggested, "and see if she hasn't got a niece who's queen of the courts there."

"How about my apartment for some prumond experiments?" Gerry offered. "I've got a new electric mixer that needs to be broken in." She made an expansive, sweeping gesture. "We'll make it a party. You're all invited."

"I'll come! I'll come!" Bettina cried with alacrity.

"Count me in as official taster," Rick said, with a lazy stretch.

"Count me out," Grandma announced emphatically. "I climbed those forty-eight steps to your apartment once, and I never expect to do it again."

"You ought to have a breeches buoy for Grandma," Bettina suggested.

As though sensing Cathy's preoccupation, Gerry turned now, wagging a finger at her. "Is it a date then for Sunday night?"

Cathy had to nod, but behind the nod was a reservation. If Rex should call— The breathtaking hope of that thought blurred her vision, so that for a moment it looked

as though Gerry was taking a blue and white tin of marshmallows from the music cabinet. She blinked. It *was* a
blue and white tin of marshmallows!

"Look what I found this afternoon while I was hunting
through Pat's music," Gerry said.

Rick sat up straight. "I remember Pat used to make a
ritual of toasting marshmallows at midnight. That's one
of the amazing things about Pat," he told Walt. "For all
his absorption and success in big business, he always had
time for such little things, too, and he always did them
in the grand manner."

"He toasted some just for me that night I had poison
ivy camping in Marin and couldn't sleep. Remember,
Cathy? We were talking about it this afternoon, only I
didn't know it was a ritual." Bettina sighed, as though
she had missed something.

"Get the long-handled fork from Cora," Gerry told
Bettina. "We've got just the right bed of coals for toasting now."

"With marshmallows two years old?" Grandma ob-
jected.

"They do look sort of petrified, but they'll toast," Gerry
said easily. She lifted the dividing waxed paper to look
at the bottom layer. Something about the way her
shoulders stiffened, the way her breath caught, made
Cathy look, too. The tiny warning signal Gerry gave her
kept her silent, made her swallow hard. It was a piece
of folded paper, and in Uncle Pat's distinctive handwriting the inscription, "For Faith alone."

What could this mean? Cathy's mind went sleuthing
through the whole evening of mystery. The neighbor's
report of a man in the shrubbery, Bettina's story of a
man on the balcony with a little white envelope. Why,
why did Uncle Pat hide a letter or whatever it was in a

box of marshmallows in the music cabinet? Did all these perplexing and unexplained things tie together? Was there possibly something mysterious, really mysterious perhaps, about the arrival of the Paris hat in its golden hatbox? Did it have a meaning other than a sentimental warning of Uncle Pat's return? Was it something that might add to Faith's bewildered hurt? A cold fear seemed to stir through her groping questions.

Glancing up from her knitting, she saw Gerry cover the box again quickly, put it back in the music cabinet with a smooth little speech about letting Pat find his marshmallows just where he had left them.

Walt said, "How about going down the hill to the drugstore with me, Cath? We could get some fresh marshmallows."

Cathy stuck her needles into her knitting and slipped into a jacket. In another second they were out on the street. They paused in front of Walt's battered jalopy.

"Maybe we'd better walk," he suggested. "Those old retreads of mine need retreading." It was a time-worn, familiar joke between them. Their arms linked as usual, and Walt's long stride adjusted to her shorter steps. But there was something disjointed between them, something troubling.

They went a way in silence, and then the old, easeful habit of confiding crowded up, blotting out everything else, and Cathy started, "You know, there's something strange going on."

"You bet there is." She knew his every trick of turbulence. Even in the dark she could sense his fists opening and closing in his pockets, the scowl on his square, freckled face. "My gosh, Cathy, you're the most changed person all of a sudden. What's come over you?"

"I didn't mean me."

"Well, I do. Here you pull the idea of wanting to be a ballet dancer out of the clear sky."

"Oh, that!" Cathy let out a deep breath. In the press of everything else she'd forgotten what a shock this would be to Walt.

"It doesn't add up. Why, only two years ago you were groaning all over the place because your grandmother had sold your Dad on the idea that all teen-age girls are awkward and a session a week of dancing school was the cure."

Cathy groaned now. "If only I'd really worked! When I think of how I skinned by with—"

"With the least possible effort," Walt filled in the gap. "And at the year's end you said it didn't really matter because your grandmother hardly knew a heel from a toe in dancing, anyway."

"But the second year I really did enjoy it."

"Seems to me I remember your cutting class to help me use the new pipe threader."

Cathy shuddered away from the mocking memory. Getting a pipe threader had been a milestone for Walt; he'd needed one so long, and Cathy's savings had been used to purchase a half interest, with a promise of a half interest in the profits of the brain child it would help construct. Her last year's absorption in the affair struck her now as utterly fantastic.

"And this year," Walt went on relentlessly, "when you had a choice of signing up for hockey or folk dancing at gym, you took folk dancing just so it would let you out of your ballet."

Once again Cathy squirmed. Her position was indefensible in the face of his tabulation. Everything he said was true; everything made sense, in a way. But, then, she'd met Rex.

They'd reached the end of the short, circular hilltop road, where they'd have to start downhill. Cathy paused, looking north through the dusky moonlit softness of fog to where the twin spires of St. Ignatius' seemed to float insubstantially in a little clearing. Turning east, the brilliant twinkling of light that was Market Street was pressed down by the fog to a soft blur, and the great bridge beyond was entirely blotted out, except for the beacons on the towers. Scenic Circle, where they stood, was an odd little street, a small, lovely, tree-rimmed hideaway with no particular district name to identify its location. Rex could have given up trying to find it, she thought. Her thoughts veered eagerly away from Walt's accusing questions, turning gratefully to this picture of Rex searching for her.

"Who is this guy from school Betts was talking about?"

"Rex Emory." There! Now it was out. "You know him."

"I know who he is. Everyone at school last year knew who *he* was." Walt's voice faltered. There was grudging respect. "But—"

"He saw me dance in the festival, and he asked me to dance with him."

"Yeah." That same doubting note deepened. One hand went up through his blond thatch in perplexity.

"He thinks I have real talent, that I ought to study ballet seriously." She paused while a wonderful wordless emotion swept over her; but when she spoke, she was surprised to hear herself sound defensive. "I was as surprised as you, at first, but I know this is what I really want to do." She paused again. The regular blasts of the Golden Gate fog horn followed by the booms from Alcatraz made a pattern of sound loud in the stillness between them. "Well, something has to happen to help you decide what career you want. Everyone can't know from the time they're born, practically, like you with your inventions."

Walt's big brown-loafered foot rubbed slowly back and forth, back and forth, crunching gravel on the pavement edge. "That's for sure." He hesitated again and then walked around in front of her, leaning back against the weathered rustic fence. "Only listen, Cath, almost every guy in the world plays a system with girls to some extent."

"You mean—they give you a line?" Cathy stood very still, aware of a bleak heaviness in her chest, her cold hands clutching her elbows in her blue-tweed jacket sleeves.

"I saw you dance at the festival."

She saw honesty struggling with kindness in his face. Honesty and kindness were integral parts of Walt. But suddenly she was wound up with words that spilled out all helter-skelter. "I guess you were surprised I didn't fall on my face; or maybe you thought because I'm left-handed I'd be left-footed, too, or dance as though I had two left feet. Or maybe you thought I'd be content to spend all of my spare time in your little world of pipes and wrenches, and now prune pits."

"I guess I just didn't think about it at all. Or maybe I just thought about you being at home looking after the kids."

"So you said this afternoon," she went on stonily. "That's what everyone thought about me." It wasn't that she minded looking after the children at home. The fact was she'd missed them terribly just these few days she had been at Faith's. What irritated her was everyone's assumption that that was all she cared about or had the ability to do.

"But some girls are just meant to be—well—home-makers, I guess. You can't help yourself if that's the way you're made."

"Well, I wasn't made just to go on clucking." As a far-off accompaniment to her words she felt a surge of nostalgic longing for the hubbub of home—the children squealing over someone hurt or calling for help to find something lost, the shouting of high spirits, their running upstairs and down, the slammed doors, the thump-thump-thump of the twins' balls against the house, the too loud TV or radio, Mee Chow's harassed pretense of scolding, the quick slithering scuff of his rope-soled shoes, the unexpected bong of his Chinese gong on special occasions that meant syrup aboil in the great copper kettle for taffy apples, her own voice coaxing, encouraging, soothing, making a game of admonishment. She swallowed tightly. "I guess I've got some real talent, too." She knew she was hitching a strange, rebellious anger to Walt, but she couldn't stop. "What if I were to say you haven't exactly set the world on fire as an inventor?"

For a second, trapped by her meanness, she felt almost sick. Oh, what's the matter with me? she wondered. If only I could forget about Rex and be my old self! Near tears, she darted a miserable upward glance at the tall boy beside her. To her relief, instead of smarting at her statement he seemed to be studying her with amusement.

"I'd say it's true so far. But it's there inside of me," he added simply. "It's like I said. If that's the way you're made, you can't help yourself. And as for prune pits— sure, it's crazy, but that's just for fast money, if it goes. Anyhow, it's no crazier than cattail cookies, and if a big impressive institution like Syracuse U can give time to such a product, I guess I can spare a few hours for prune pits."

Silently Cathy ceded him a point, giving him an uncomfortable sidelong glance. If there was sarcasm in his words, there was none in his tone, none in his expression. "You know there's always a time when you have to step up to bat and take a whack at any pitch that comes along." There was his engaging grin. Unexpectedly he reached for her hand. "If you really want to be a ballet dancer, more power to you, but I don't want you to get hurt, Lefty." This was his pet name, reserved for rare occasions. His prolonged gaze held hers, as if he were measuring her with new knowledge added to sixteen years of friendship.

"Maybe there's something inside of me you don't know anything about." She withdrew her hand, half-turning away, living again all the frustration at school when she'd felt so left out of glamorous career talk, when she'd felt so stupidly in-between-ish, as she'd put it to Gerry. And then dimly she was aware of another emotion—the self-doubt that Rex's failure to appear had evoked. In the midst of her anger she had an impulse to tell Walt about her disappointment. She turned back toward him. The weird planes of a cypress twisted by the Pacific winds stood out behind and above him, framing his height, his breadth. The square, honest ruggedness of his being seemed a match for nature. Little jewel drops of fog glistened on his light hair. It would have been impossible not to feel admiration; but as swiftly as it had come, pride dismissed the impulse to confide her disappointment.

Instead, she said, "It isn't as though I were the kind of person who has a yen for twenty different kinds of careers." She thought of the girls at school with their on-again off-again, erratic ideas of becoming first a dress designer, then a movie star, and then an airline hostess. In a sudden revelation she told herself that maybe deciding on a career is a little like falling in love. They say that if you're the type who doesn't do it easily, when you fall you fall harder.

She lifted her head to the sky. Her breath caught. Like a shooting star plummeting straight through her from high, high in the space of dark, night sky came the question: Am I in love with Rex? Is this what it's really like? Miss Allison and Gerry had labeled it "hero worship." Wasn't that the way she'd thought of it herself? How could you tell? The sound of his name being spoken, the way she felt about him, about his dancing, was different from any other sound or feeling she'd ever experienced. Certainly it was on another plane from what she felt for Walt. Walt—familiar, dependable—yes, lovable. But loving and being in love surely weren't synonymous?

A sudden gust of wind blustering through her hair and rippling Walt's blond thatch brought her out of her silent questioning.

"I'm just wondering," Walt challenged, "if you really go in for this career, and if you had to choose some time, like, say, one of the twins had the double pip, and yet you knew you had to go dance somewhere with this guy—"

"That kind of a question isn't fair," Cathy replied helplessly.

"Lots of things in life aren't what you'd call fair, but you still have to choose."

It was clear enough what Walt expected her to say. It was what the whole family would expect. Her chin lifted, but to her secret chagrin her spirits refused to match the movement. "I guess I know how I'd choose," she said half-defiantly. "It wouldn't be so hard." But she meant that it would be terribly hard. How could she choose?

Walt's gaze continued unyielding. "O.K.," he said easily, maddeningly. "We'll see."

Cathy turned away and began to walk quickly back to the house in uncertain resistance. It didn't make sense after what was practically a quarrel, her first with Walt, to be thinking, I must ask him to put up a practice *barre* for me when I get home. It didn't make sense at all. But Walt would do it. Walt had never refused her anything.

5

The Stolen Letter

WAKING EARLY THE NEXT MORNING, the first thought in Cathy's mind was the reprieving memory of Rex searching for her house and not finding it. It was so much nicer to believe than that he simply hadn't come.

Grandma, Gerry, and Rick, worn out by waiting, had gone home at last, and the house had settled down to exhausted sleep. A sweep of sadness for Faith passed over Cathy, for no excuse could be made for Uncle Pat. He simply hadn't arrived.

Now her arms scooped aside the blue-silk quilt, circled her head on the matching blue pillow; her eyes closed against the first pale shafts of daylight, and she drifted away on the delight of daydreaming. At home this early hour was the only time she had for the privacy of day-dreaming. Now here, in the luxury of this lofty, high-ceilinged room, with its bleached-walnut furniture, filmy blue draperies, blue rugs, and a love of a corner fireplace, that inner world of wishing seemed even more appropriate.

"In a minute," she told herself, "I'll get up and do my dance exercises." Mentally she put her muscles through first position, with heels touching, toes turned out, then moved her feet apart for a second, now pulling the right foot back to the left, bringing the right heel against the left instep for third position. Standing outside herself she saw the classical straightness of her knees, moved along to see her thumb and third finger indented, her hand in line with her arm, yet relaxed, drifting. "Very nice," she seemed to hear Rex say approvingly, and, "that's just the feeling—" The words of tribute he'd uttered there on the school stage repeated themselves in the stillness with tantalizing clarity in her memory. And with them came something else, something clamoring, something so illuminating that she sat straight up in bed, goose pimples starting down her back—the picture, picked out in detail now, of him scribbling Faith's address on a scrap of paper, stuffing it carelessly into his pocket.

Of course that was it. He could have lost that scrap of paper. It could have fallen out when he'd reached in for change or while he was dancing. She hugged herself with sudden glee, the goose pimples fading as quickly as they had come. Even if he'd wanted to look up her number in the phone book he couldn't, because he'd remember that she was to be at her aunt's and he wouldn't know Faith's name.

Why, in a case like this it was absolutely all right to call him. She simply had to, she reassured herself triumphantly, arguing against Gerry's advice that would try to sneak in its frosty warning to spoil everything.

For a moment the tide of supreme happiness she'd known yesterday in anticipation of her date with Rex welled within her, and then, because her thoughts could never really be separated from her family for very long, she began to think about Bettina, and oddly her spirits began a steady descent. A formless, vague worry gnawed at her, tied up with last night's mystery. Although the tale that Bettina had told of what had frightened her on the balcony dovetailed with the neighbor's account of seeing a man in the shrubbery, Cathy knew that her curious feeling of disturbance was now focused on her first reaction to Bettina's story, on her certainty that Bettina hadn't been telling the truth.

Leaning on the bed table, she looked across to the small cocoon of Bettina's sleeping figure in the twin bed. The smooth, young, rosy brow, the angelic imperturbability of expression said nothing. Oh, bother, she thought, why do I have to start inventing troubles? Why can't I just concentrate on Rex? She squeezed her eyes shut, but the ecstasy would not be recaptured; the apprehension, the suspicion overlapped everything else, seeming to draw her gaze again, almost against her will, to her sleeping sister.

Now she knew what it was. In that first glance something had registered dimly. Something was out of place, her eyes seeing it, as she anxiously tried to get back to her half-waking daydreams, not seeing it. She got out of bed and stood over Bettina, her fingers reaching out to touch the fold of a small, creamy white envelope just visible under the edge of the blue pillow slip, twin to the one she'd been sleeping on.

"Bettina!" Cathy's voice had its firmest no-nonsense quality.

Bettina's long, inky lashes lifted, her hand going in half sleep to the envelope under her pillow.

"What are you hiding? What's that letter?"

Only Bettina's eyes answered with anguished fright. For a drawn-out minute there was only the sound of their heavy breathing in the still summer air, the silken swish of the diaphanous draperies billowing and flattening in the early summer morning breeze. "I took it." Cornered, Bettina's speech was barely audible. "I didn't mean to. I just meant to look at the Paris hat. There wasn't any man on Faith's balcony. But when the lady next door called and said there was someone hiding in the shrubbery, it seemed like a good way to explain the letter being gone." Bettina ran out of breath. She drew the envelope from under her pillow, handed it to Cathy. "I didn't read it," she concluded.

Cathy saw the single word "Faith" written on the envelope in Uncle Pat's bold, unmistakable handwriting. It was sealed and obviously hadn't been opened. She pulled the blue quilt from her bed, wrapped herself in it and sat beside Bettina. "Now start over and tell me slowly just how you got this."

"I was on the balcony looking into Faith's room. She wasn't there, and all I wanted was a look at the Paris hat. Why, my goodness! She hadn't even opened the golden hatbox. It was on the dressing table right by the French doors, and I reached in and just lifted the lid enough for a peek, and I was getting the tissue paper out of the way and then I heard Faith coming back, so I had to pull my hand out quickly, and I don't know how it happened, but my hand had this letter in it." Bettina sat up in bed, leaning forward earnestly. "It was the craziest thing, because it was just like my hand didn't belong to me and didn't know what it was doing. You could've knocked me over with a soap bubble when I saw what I was holding. That's the truth, so help me!" She crossed the pocket of her pink polka-dotted pajamas that covered her heart.

In spite of the first shock Cathy felt touched by the genuine perplexity in Bettina's expression. Outrage crumbled into uncertainty. Things like this did happen once in a while. Her anger lashing out at Walt last night was almost in the same class; for in a way her tongue hadn't seemed to belong to her as she said hateful things she hadn't meant and wouldn't have said if she hadn't been goaded by some inner force beyond her control.

"I know," she said softly. "I got mad at Walt last night—I didn't really mean to—now I have to apologize."

Relieved breath whooshed out of Bettina as she obviously took comfort from Cathy's reflective expression. "Oh, Cathy, it's such a relief to tell someone! I've been so frightened and I felt so sneaky. I couldn't put the letter back in the box because Faith was right in her room, and I stuck it down my neck and tightened my belt so it wouldn't slip through. But it kept burning me all evening, like I had a red-hot coal or something down my front, and when you were trying to make me tell what I'd seen on the balcony I was scared green you'd hear the crackling under my shirt, and that's why I had to do a fast belly flop on the bear rug."

Bettina had suffered, Cathy mused.

"Do you think I'm going to be one of those klepto—somethings or other? Am I going to have an irresistible impulse to swipe things right and left?"

"Don't be an idiot!" Cathy banished the glint in Bettina's eyes with a thoroughly businesslike edge to her tone that admitted no argument. "And there's no use getting dramatic now, either. You've done something terribly wrong, and you've got to set it right. You've got to march right in to Faith now."

"Oh, I couldn't!" Bettina huddled down under the covers. "I just couldn't. I'd rather—rather sit in a nest of tarantulas," she rushed on, carried away by her own words.

"We're fresh out of tarantulas," Cathy informed her. "So there's no choice." Cathy pulled back the bedclothes. "Up and into your robe."

"I was hoping I could slip it back into the box when Faith was out of her room."

"Uh-*uh!* You hoped wrong. You're going to hand it to her right now." Underneath her briskness Cathy's own spirit flinched. Faith's elusive dreaminess might cover a core of anger really formidable. Still waters often did run deep. But Bettina couldn't be allowed to get away with this.

Bettina had another idea. The slow-motion tying of her pink-flannel bathrobe sash stopped altogether. "Here's something we haven't thought about. Even if there wasn't any man on Faith's balcony, there was one hiding in the bushes. Mrs. Brownlee next door saw him, and Rick saw his footprints. Remember? Who do you suppose it was? And what was he doing?"

Cathy finished shrugging into her own robe, thinking about the mystery. "I don't know. But come on now— you're just trying to sidetrack me."

"Maybe it was Uncle Pat. Maybe he came home and heard Grandma blowing off steam and got scared and went away again."

"Don't be ridic! Nothing would scare Uncle Pat. Here." She held out the letter.

Unwillingly Bettina's limp hand accepted the envelope. "It's too early," she insisted. "Faith won't be awake." As Cathy's eyes sought the clock with uncertainty, Bettina pushed her advantage. "Let's get our tennis racquets and practice our drives against the garage wall."

"I'm not going to be playing tennis," Cathy told her. "Dancing muscles have to be trained in other ways."

Bettina's black bangs flipped with the vehemence of her emotion. "Well, I think it was absolutely rotten of Rex not even to phone you last night. The dope! That was the least he—Say, maybe he was the man in the bushes. Maybe he could have been just about to ring the doorbell and heard Grandma roar and was scared he'd been seen. So he hid a few minutes to be sure no one came out to drag him in."

"That's another silly idea," Cathy said very loudly to drown out the still voice that said it could be true. It just possibly could. But how much easier, how much more comforting, it was to believe that he'd lost her address than to think that he'd actually been at the door and been scared off or just plain horrified by Grandma's scolding voice.

Bettina propped the pilfered letter against the blue-shaded lamp on the night table. "Let's go look at those footprints Rick found. Maybe there are some clues— you know, a button or something like that. They're always finding them in mystery stories." She scampered ahead, her pink bunny scuffies flapping down the stairs, as she whispered a running fire of possibilities. Cathy, following, felt her knees quiver uncontrollably. Then a tide of drenching relief washed over her as they looked at the footprints and saw that they were far too large to have been made by Rex's slender, dancing feet.

Thankfully Cathy breathed in the cool, moist earth smell, the faint fragrance of rhododendrons budding into blossom, the early morning freshness. From the back of the house they heard the screen door slam, Cora's industinct voice urging Jimbo out, and then the tearing, rollicking whish of his furry body as he tore around the house with his chewing shoe in his mouth and found them.

"Hey, look out!" Bettina admonished. "You're spoiling our evidence." She patted the dog affectionately and tried to direct him through an opening in the shrubbery, but Jimbo, shoe discarded, lay on his back, paws waving in the air, his tongue lolling, sundappled and joyfully dripping. "Now he's done it. He's right on top of our best footprint," she grunted, prying the dog's unwilling body up. "In mystery movies they always have a police guard around the footprints, and then they make a plaster cast, and later the guilty person's shoe fits exactly."

"Well, this isn't a movie," Cathy reminded.

"Maybe Jimbo made these prints with his play shoe."

"No dog, not even Jimbo," Cathy pointed out, "could set a shoe down several times in the earth exactly right to make such definite prints."

"But it is a mystery, and a footprint is always a red-hot clue. And you said yourself you heard someone cough or sneeze out here. Come on, let's look. Maybe there's a shred of someone's coat or something. Oh, golly! I've just had a brilliant flash." Her voice squeaked with rushing excitement. "You know what this could be? It could be someone who knows that Uncle Pat is coming home with sacks and sacks of diamonds and he's waiting to hold him up."

"How do we know Uncle Pat's even bringing diamonds?"

"But, Cathy, it could be just what I said. Why would anyone be hiding in these bushes? Come on and look," she insisted.

In spite of the feeling that Bettina was letting her imagination run away with her, Cathy found herself

caught up by the idea. Searching the area with Bettina
for clues, she thought suddenly of that other mystery, the
one Bettina had missed, when Gerry had swiftly closed
the marshmallow box and put it away. There had been a
curiously unfathomable expression on Gerry's face as she
had flashed the brief warning glance that had kept Cathy
from asking questions. Cathy's scalp prickled. She could
go in right now and look in the marshmallow box. But if
she did, wouldn't she be just as bad as Bettina peeking
into Faith's hatbox? Gerry's glance had plainly said,
"This is none of our business." She shook herself as
persistent curiosity snaked back again and met the horrid
remembrance of Pandora's box, that myth, ancient and
warning, which she'd quoted often enough to her young
brothers and sisters. Behind her Bettina complained,
"Well, all I've found is a candy bar wrapper I threw
away yesterday."

Cathy's mind switched to the other overlapping
mystery. Fantastic as it sounded, Bettina's theory of a
diamond thief had some merit. Confused and shivering,
Cathy stepped from the bushes, glad for the warmth of
the ardent morning sunshine. She decided then to call
Gerry at her office. But first she would phone Rex.
Thinking of her call to Rex suddenly gave Cathy a sensation so light-hearted that she agreed readily to go along
with Bettina while she returned the letter to Faith.

Indoors they went directly to Faith's room. Cathy
hadn't realized how beautiful Faith was until this moment, when her eyes traveled over the exquisite curve of
Faith's cheek, the pale gold of her long hair on the white
pillow. How perfectly she was complemented by the
almost theatrical decor of gold and white—a result of
Uncle Pat's planning—the dull-gold lamps with chalky-
white shades, the antiqued-gold mirror frame and the

mirror itself reflecting the white carpet, the gilt cabinet that held Uncle Pat's jade collection, the great white bed, and lastly the golden heart-shaped hat box on the white flounced dressing table near the French windows! As Cathy sat on the low slipper chair with its white velvet cushions, she couldn't help thinking irrelevantly of what would become of white velvet cushions at home with the twins and their everlastingly taffy-appled hands. Then all at once she returned to the scene before her as Bettina blinked back tears and concluded her confession.

It was obvious that Faith hadn't opened the hatbox or she would have seen the letter before Bettina had taken it. The existence of a letter was a shock to her—a shock that stunned her to silence. Then slowly, almost fearfully, she drew the folded paper from the envelope. From where Cathy sat, she could see that it contained a brief line. Finally, softly, as though waking from sleep, Faith was reading aloud, a catch in her voice, "Will see you next week. Love, Pat."

A whole week to wait. But strangely Faith didn't seem to mind. "Why, she's almost relieved," Cathy mused. "It can't be indifference—no one could be indifferent to Uncle Pat. What did it mean then?"

Bettina stood close to the bed, still taut, still tearful. "Am I—am I forgiven?" The words were choked.

"Of course." Faith touched her gently, a tentative caress, so different from the swooping hug Gerry would have given, but with a world of meaning just the same.

"Could we see the Paris hat?" Bettina asked, smiling on a breath of relief. As Faith nodded and smiled, Bettina, in her impeding scuffies, flapped over to the heart box, had the hat out of its tissues in a trice, and held it up in wonder. Fragile straw lace, wide brim, shallow crown, a simple blue-velvet band, it was such utter per-

fection that Cathy caught her breath. And when Bettina
placed it on Faith's head, holding back the silky stream
of pale-gold hair, Cathy gasped again. She picked up
the gold-backed, monogramed mirror from the dressing
table and held it close for Faith to see her own reflection.

"Oh, it's lovely, lovely!" Bettina cried. "I wish I looked
just like you."

Faith said, "But you look just like Gerry—Gipsy face
and ways." She sighed. "Oh, if we could all be like
Gerry!"

If we just could, Cathy thought, putting the mirror
back on the dressing table. Aloud she said, "Everything's
been so easy for Gerry. She's so talented. That's just
what I said to Gerry yesterday," she told them in sudden
recollection, "but Gerry said, 'Talent isn't everything.' "

"It may not be everything, but it sure helps," Bettina
pointed out forthrightly. "If I could only draw like
Gerry!"

"She's worked, though," Faith reminded. "You know,
she even went to medical school to take anatomy because
she wasn't satisfied with the course they gave in art
school. When she draws a figure, she knows just where
every bone and muscle lies beneath the skin."

Bettina said, "I know. She told me we've got something
like two hundred bones in us." Then abandoning the
subject and yielding to curiosity, she asked the question
all had pondered. "Faith, are you glad Uncle Pat's coming back? Are you?" She leaned against the bed, a
reverent finger tracing the lace pattern in the straw of
the Paris hat still on Faith's head.

In the silence it was hard to tell what Faith might be
thinking behind the shuttering of her eyes. "Yes," she
breathed at last. "I've longed for it to happen—" There
was a special note in her voice, a kind of special loving-

ness. "And yet—I guess I've been a little afraid." She went on, slowly searching for words as though she'd forgotten her audience. "I think Pat had a picture of the ideal wife he wanted me to fit instantly. He's so intense, and I've been such a dreamer. I was only half there, only half-seeing and half-touching all the things he cares about so fully."

Cathy saw the quick pulse at the base of Faith's throat, the little droop of wistful sadness that gave way to an odd, trembling laugh. "I had to think of things for months first, while Pat was always out and doing."

That was right. Cathy thought of the things waiting in the den—the clothes gathered for the foreign mission orphans but never packed or shipped and the unfinished hooked rug for the church bazaar, the bazaar long since past; of Faith's irregular attendance at Red Cross meetings; of other half-finished projects that filled Faith's days; and now the way she'd put off opening the Paris hatbox. Cathy sensed Faith reproaching herself deeply, relentlessly. That, too, was hard to understand; for most wives would simply blame their husbands for leaving. But could Faith change?

"Can I change?" Cathy asked herself. "Can I switch from being a mother hen to concentrating on a career?" The question burned in a bright haze that once again included Rex, his lean darkness and arresting grace vivid in her recognizing vision. "I want to dance with you again, Rex," her heart cried. And her mind said, "I've got to be worthy." Again she heard Miss Allison saying, "Set your sights high, but face your limitations squarely." It was kind, sensible, well-meant counsel.

What is the trouble with Faith? She wants to be a good wife. Cathy shook her head in silent puzzlement.

Is it timidity? Self-doubt? Procrastination? "Ineffectual" was the word Gerry had used.

Mercurial as always, Bettina now went bounding away from Faith's grown-up talk. "I guess I'm glad I look like Gerry." There was a cheerful frankness in her voice. "But Cathy looks a little like you, Faith. She's getting tall and her eyes are gray." She studied her sister with artless candor. "If only her hair were blond instead of reddish-brown."

"But I'm not like Faith," Cathy denied silently. Not that she'd mind being as enchantingly beautiful as Faith. But in every other way she didn't like the comparison at all. She'd ten times rather have Gerry's verve for living, her well-organized mind, her talents. "I'm not a dazey dreamer like Faith," she assured herself firmly. "I'm not a bit like her. I'm the kind of person who does something about her problem." She stood up with resolution. "And right now, too."

6

Telephone Call
To Telegraph Hill

BY MID-MORNING Cathy had put in a satisfying period of dance practice. At least her muscle-aching diligence was cause for satisfaction. She had done *pliés* in four positions for nearly an hour, stretching tendons and muscles in feet and legs, and then had moved on to *jetés,* to *arabesques,* to *battements frappés* and *battements tendus.* This was fun, really fun, and she was getting better; even her turn-out was better, Cathy decided silently, addressing a world brilliant with the prospect of phoning Rex. Once she had been interrupted by Cora, pausing with her vacuum to say, "If you'll forgive me for speaking plain, all that twisting and jumping doesn't look like dancing to me."

But Cathy just smiled a radiant smile, her outer eye on

the clock, her inner eye on the beckoning privacy of the drugstore phone booth where she'd make her call to Rex at ten o'clock. Surely anyone, even a ballet dancer, would be up and available at that hour.

Just as she was about to leave, the phone in the hall rang. When Cora called her, she picked up the instrument with such a sudden roaring in her ears that her father's deep, familiar voice saying that he was going to Chicago to attend a medical convention sounded as though it were coming through a filter of dense fog. Bettina came running through the hall, clamoring to speak to Daddy, too. In a jumble of shame at wishing that it had been Rex instead of her father calling and relief at having Bettina occupied while she got away by herself to the drugstore, she shot out of the house.

It seemed a good omen that the rear of the drugstore held no customers, that the phone booth was unoccupied. She had already looked up Rex's number and had it and his address on a slip of paper. The very sight of the digits in their proper sequence and the knowledge that the moment after she dialed them she would actually be speaking to Rex produced a tingling weakness up and down her spine. But what, a last warning voice seemed to counsel, if Rex really hadn't lost the address? What if he just doesn't want to see you, to have you dance with him again? What if all the nice things he said are simply a line, as Walt suspected? So what! She answered the accusing questions. So I'll find out. That's all there is to it. But no amount of will power beaming her thoughts in this casual direction could keep her hands from shaking uncontrollably.

She dialed the second and third numbers. The small enclosure with its feeble overhead light grew sickeningly hot. The odor of stale cigar smoke and drug store chemicals surged around her. She stood up from the small seat, leaned her forehead against the cool pebbly metal surface of the wall, and studied the tattered telephone book on its chain. The front cover was elaborately decorated with penciled doodlings, including heart-enclosed initials somehow richly connotative of all she was going through.

She quickly dialed the final numbers, heard the ring in Rex's home. At the same time a man and a woman converged on her. While the phone continued to ring, the man gave a hasty, disgruntled glance and turned away, but the woman, middle-aged, stout, with dime in impatient hand, stood just outside the phone-booth door and stared at her as though hoping to reduce chatty conversation to a minimum by the very force of her nearness.

Cathy turned her back slightly, ran her tongue over her lips, and heard her voice ask for Rex in response to a woman's voice saying hello. "Just a moment," the voice replied.

For a moment Cathy hesitated. She could just hang up and go home and be free to go beaching with Bettina. She thought of the cool, buffeting froth of a Pacific wave washing over her after the delight of running across sun-baked sand. And then suddenly she was practically jumping out of her clammy skin at a sharp rap on the phone-booth door. "Are you using that phone?" The impatient voice of the stout woman came, muffled, through the glass.

"I'm waiting," Cathy started to answer the woman through the door. Then, aware that a voice was finally on the other end of the line and that she'd been yelling into the phone, she apologized. "Oh, I'm sorry. Hello! Hello, Rex?"

"This is Rex's sister Rachel. Who's calling?"

"Catherine Darfield." There was a pause that seemed indefinably hostile. Then some flash of insight prompted her to explain. "Rex was coming to rehearse a dance with me last night. He talked to me about it at school. I thought maybe he lost my address or something—" She broke off nervously, scarcely breathing.

Rachel said, "Oh, yes. I remember."

The very unexpectedness of this remark unnerved Cathy even further, so that her voice scaled upward in unnatural shrillness. "You mean Rex told you about me?"

"Well, I didn't quite remember your name."

The friendly tone of Rachel's voice sent a wave of relief through Cathy. Rachel added, "Rex had to go to Hollywood to dance in a picture for TV."

An energizing breeze seemed to fill the little telephone cubicle. He hadn't forgotten her! He'd only been called away on a professional engagement. "How wonderful!" she managed.

"He'll only be gone a week or so. I know the dance he had in mind, so why don't you come over and I'll get you started."

Obviously, then, Rachel was a dancer, too. And obviously it was intended—planned in heaven—that she should really dance with Rex again.

"Come Monday afternoon." Rachel seemed to be consulting a time schedule. "Two o'clock would be fine. We're on Telegraph Hill, you know."

"Two o'clock will be perfect," Cathy assured her. "And I have your address."

Happiness cascading in ever larger waves encompassed Cathy and everything in the store around her. The stout lady, now examining hot-water bottles, was bathed in it. "That's a nice one," Cathy informed her remotely, touching the red rubber. Her feet on the sidewalk outside danced with a resiliency that seemed to have nothing to do with ordinary locomotion. The dazzling dreams for the future were conjured into existence again by just the few words that Rachel had spoken, and she smiled in the direction of Hollywood—and Rex.

On a street corner she stopped to let traffic pass. The morning sun was warm on her hair, and the morning breeze fanned her full skirt. Overhead the same breeze fanned the upward flight of a flock of gulls. Dreamily she fancied that the waves of her happiness melted into the wind's updraft, helping the birds in their effortless soaring.

But like all soaring joy this needed to be shared. Bettina, for all her closeness, was just too young. Gerry! Of course, Gerry was the perfect confidant. Just being with her meant gaiety, shared laughter, and enthusiastic attentive interest in whatever you talked about. Cathy had wanted to call Gerry, anyway, about the marshmallow box. Now, as she skimmed along, she decided to phone Gerry at her office. Maybe they could have lunch together at their favorite restaurant in Maiden Lane, just the two of them. She began to hurry, planning what she would wear.

In the room she shared with Bettina, Cathy found her sister scrubbed and rosy, in her own best outfit, intent on braiding green ribbons in her hair. "This is Cora's afternoon off, and I'm going with her to visit Bessie—you know, her niece with the two sets of twins."

"The one who was going to dance the high fandango on the elephant's back," they ended up in an amused chorus.

"How did this happen?" Speculatively Cathy moved the hangers that held things in the closet, finally selecting her gray gabardine suit.

Uneasy embarrassment replaced Bettina's merriment. "I thought I'd feel better if I told everyone about the letter that I took out of the hatbox. I thought it was the least I could do. Cora really blew her cork. Said I'd put everyone through a fiendish nightmare of waiting. If Faith had known Uncle Pat wasn't coming for a week, we could have all settled down. Honestly, I've never seen Cora really mad before." She flipped back the braids. "You've heard of people who quivered like Jell-O?"

Cathy's head emerged from her best sweater. "I've heard," she admitted indulgently.

"Well, she picked up the waffle iron, and I thought she was going to hit me with it, and I closed my eyes." Bettina's eyes squeezed tight, re-creating the scene. "Because actually I knew I deserved it."

"Goose!" Cathy chided gently. "How could she hit you with a waffle iron?"

"She could," Bettina insisted. "Haven't you ever noticed what a powerful arm Cora's got? But she just slammed it on the drainboard and began to clean it like fury. And after a while she seemed to have worked off her mad, because she mixed up some wonderful batter and made us each a three-decker waffle sandwich with ham and honey."

"Poor Cora!" Cathy shook her head. "She'll never really start that diet."

"Anyway, while we were eating was when she invited me to go see Bessie. Not that seeing twins is such a thrill when we've got them at home every day."

"But two sets in one family is a nice novelty," Cathy said.

"I wonder how our twins are getting along? That was a neat idea of the camp counselor to stick them in separate cabins, only I wonder if they miss each other as well as their fights."

"I miss them," Cathy surprised herself by saying.

"Do you? Honestly?" The eager entreaty in Bettina's voice was just as surprising as the very real wave of homesickness for the children that Cathy experienced.

"Of course, I do."

"You've been so far away, either dancing dream dances on pink clouds with Rex or glooming like a mooley-cow with a—"

"With a migraine." Cathy supplied the alliteration with a wry grin.

"What *do* you think about when you're dancing dream dances on pink clouds with Rex?" Bettina asked.

"Why, dream dancing. What else?" Cathy responded hungrily to the chance to talk about Rex. "And as for pink clouds—well, actually, you really do have to give a thought to them, too. At least to what's around you." She went on happily thinking aloud, recalling Rex's words. "In choreography—that is, dance composition—there's the all-over design which must be satisfying and lovely from every angle. And then there's something called the air pattern which is especially important for the audience viewing you from above."

Bettina nodded knowingly. "You mean the cheap seats in the balcony."

Cathy smiled at Bettina's graphic expression, ran the hairbrush upward through her hair with such vigor that her scalp tingled. Possibly she hadn't used the right words or conveyed the exact meaning of Rex's explanation, but a second later she saw that it didn't matter. Her sister's thoughts were miles away.

"But don't you ever think about us any more? About the kids at camp?"

"I couldn't forget my very own family." But she had
—not forgotten exactly, but pushed back. And now they
all came crowding forward, eagerly, clamoringly alive. "I
hope they're not just letting Tess sit around and read all
day."

"My gosh, yes," Bettina agreed. "What Tess needs is to
learn to throw a ball—any kind of ball. And if they can
just make Pipper stop skinning out of his pajamas after
he gets in bed. . . . Honestly, Cathy, you've got to put
your foot down. It's disgusting the way he likes fresh air
all over him. Even if he is only five, it's time—"

"I'm sure Tess will be able to identify more wild flowers
and birds than anyone there."

"She'll be the only kid at camp who can give a tail-to-
topknot description of a ferruginous hawk or any other
bird you want to name. If they can just get her to play
some games instead of grubbing around in the woods all
day for rare specimens of marsh milkwort or something!"

Cathy took a long look at Bettina. She has all my old
worries. It's not right. She's only twelve. "I'll tell you
what," she said impulsively, "tomorrow we'll go to the
beach for the whole day, just the two of us. We'll rent
surfboards."

"Oh, Cathy! Could we—could we be just like we used
to be?" Her light smile wavered. "I guess we could be if
—if Rex doesn't call. Huh?" She bent over quickly to pull
at a sock that had wadded down in her sneaker.

"He won't be calling for a week or so. He's out of
town." Briefly Cathy explained her phone conversation
with Rachel and her plan now to surprise Gerry at her
office. But if Rex did call, she questioned herself, if he
got back unexpectedly early and did call—an arm half in
her jacket sleeve jammed there, and the familiar faintness
caught her. Suddenly she felt annoyed. "I'm going to

quit even thinking about Rex. I'll just quit," she vowed fiercely, jerking at her jacket. "I'll practice and take lessons and dance, but I won't go through all this agony. It's silly. Maybe even trying to be a dancer is silly. I've got too much to do at home."

The recent conversation about the children at camp sent her mind jumping ahead to the way every circumstance in her life would have to change. She began to regret her impetuosity in announcing her ambition so firmly.

She opened her mouth to speak; then closed it again, biting her cheek as she caught sight of her new pink ballet slippers on her bedside chair. Instantly the dull heaviness her vow had produced, the dread prospect of sinking back to the status of an in-between-ish person, with no plans for a career, lifted. Certainly she was going to dance. To still the rising giddiness, she forced her attention back to Bettina. "Maybe you can get Bessie to do her high fandango without the elephant."

"Whatever the high fandango is," Bettina said.

Cathy slipped the buckle tongue in the last eyelet of her suede belt. "Matter of fact, I feel a little ashamed. I always thought Bessie and her two sets of twins was one of Cora's figments, along with whale flipper from Alaska."

"Whatever figments are." Bettina repeated the form of her questioning comment.

"Figments," Cathy considered, "are fibs that ought to be labeled fiction. Like your whopper of a man on Faith's balcony yesterday."

Bettina's face screwed up in a truculent pucker. "But don't forget there *was* a man in the shrubbery—a diamond thief." Inspired imagining as always kindled the dancing spark in her eyes again.

"A what?"

"Well," Bettina, brought to earth, amended, "anyway, there was a man because we saw his footprints, and he might have been a diamond thief. And since Uncle Pat won't be home right away, don't you think we ought to tell the police? Don't you?"

"I'll ask Gerry," Cathy answered finally. She took a few slips of blue agathea from a little crystal vase on the dressing table, carefully made a boutonnière and slipped it into her lapel buttonhole. Then, with a last glance in the mirror, she revolved, arms in fifth position, before Bettina, not so much for approval as to satisfy the lovely, vapory ache to dance. Her steps took her out to the hall.

Bettina ran after her. "Wait, wait!" Eyes downcast, she hunched against the banister. "I called Grandma, too, and told her about the letter."

Cathy gave her sister an approving pat, moved by her obvious contrition but understanding, too, the need for true relief that comes with wholesale confession.

"Grandma wasn't mad at all. She just said, 'M-m-m!' and 'Hmph!' And she said she was going to bed and would like not to be disturbed for anything short of earthquake or fire."

"Probably tired out," Cathy commented. "Grandma put in a pretty strenuous night." She pulled up Bettina's small pointed chin affectionately. "Have fun at Bessie's."

7

Luncheon in Maiden Lane

GERRY BENT OVER the drawing board, her arm moving in quick, sure strokes. The Harlequin uptilt of her shell-rimmed glasses added a piquant touch to the planes of her face. The firm outline of dark, rosy cheek and even the way she moved her head were revealingly young. She looked more like nineteen than twenty-five, Cathy observed admiringly.

Cathy turned her attention back to the pile of fashion sketches in her lap. "I'll be through in a jiffy," Gerry had promised, "and then we'll go to lunch." The jiffy had stretched to nearly half an hour of absorbed work, but Cathy didn't mind. There was a fascination about this small island of quiet that was Gerry's private domain in the big, scurrying, typewriter-clicking office of the advertising agency for which Gerry worked. Cathy relished the smell of inks and paint and turpentine, the clutter of brushes and pencils and cardboard, the contagious feeling of accomplishment that watching the magic of Gerry's fingers produced.

Cathy understood exactly what Faith had meant when she said that Gerry knew every bone and muscle under the folds of a garment. Without a single irrelevant stroke Gerry drew naturalness in every turn of the high-fashion figures, a naturalness overlaid with her own mood and humor.

The door opened, and an older man came in with some sheets of lettering. "Will you O.K. these, Miss Farrell?"

Gerry jumped up from her own work. Head cocked to one side, slender shoulders square in a raspberry-silk shirt, hands plunged into the pockets of her straight black skirt, she gave each page careful scrutiny. Her final nod seemed breezy, even casual, but Cathy sensed that the work had measured up to absolute technical perfection. When the man had gone, Gerry stretched. "How about a brisk walk to Maiden Lane and our favorite restaurant?"

"I was hoping you'd say that," Cathy told her. "That's just what I had in mind." Glancing at the work on the drawing board while Gerry got her coat and hat, Cathy said in puzzlement, "What's this? It looks, well, kind of half there."

"It's actually only a third there," Gerry explained. "It's what they call a color-separation job. When it comes out in one of the big, glossy fashion magazines, it will be printed in three colors."

"But there isn't any color here at all. It's just black ink."

Gerry nodded. "That's right. The artist's job is to make a separate sketch outlining where each color will go. Then the engraver makes a plate for each color. It'll be run through the press for green in this case, go back in the press for yellow, and then the last time for magenta.

The printings are done one on top of another. Then when you get the finished product, you have all three colors in their proper places. And if the printing isn't exact and there's a blurred effect, it's called being out of register." She grimaced. "And woe betide anyone who turns out that kind of sloppy work!"

"I had no idea just printing a picture of a dress could be so complicated."

"Any craft or art seems complicated until you understand the technique, and then," Gerry continued, linking arms companionably and leading Cathy out to the elevator, "all you have to do is practice until you're just a grade above topnotch, your product is uniformly predictable, and you're a success. Howling success," she tacked on, with a twinkle, "is the phrase preferred by some."

"That's almost what Rex said about becoming a professional dancer." They turned up Powell Street, past the cable-car turntable, with the clacking slap of the cables in their slot, past great jars of lavender, pink, and purple stocks that poured out their spicy fragrance from sidewalk flower stands. Both girls clutched their hats as they bent against the prevailing San Francisco wind.

Gerry's throaty, knowing "m-m-m" was interested, inviting confidence. "You've been shining all over since you burst into my office, so I take it you've heard from Rex."

"Not exactly—" Cathy broke off as a young man fell into step with them. He was someone Gerry knew from the advertising world, who, in spite of Gerry's tactful maneuvering, persisted in walking along with them and talking shop about a dog biscuit account for which he was angling.

As they turned their backs on the St. Francis Hotel to cut through Union Square, Cathy's thoughts drifted to

the intriguing legend that the St. Francis washed all its
change daily so that the nickels and dimes and quarters
one got in change there gleamed. Under the conversation about dog biscuits she recalled Uncle Pat's taking
her to lunch there years ago in the fabulous dining room
and how eager she'd been at the end of the meal for a
glimpse of the change on the waiter's little silver tray.
But although she had been disappointed, there had been
a sense of inestimable pride in the grand way in which
Uncle Pat had waved the change aside before the waiter
had had a chance to put it down. That had been years
ago—before her mother had died. Now an echo of that
far-away happy time joined the happiness that was today,
the starry feeling that was knowing Rex and planning a
career, the very special feeling of expectancy that was
the homecoming of Uncle Pat.

When they were finally alone and seated in the little
restaurant, their orders given, Gerry said, "By the way,
Bettina phoned to tell me about that letter in Faith's hatbox."

"She did go in for self-punishment, didn't she?"

"Self-punishment is always the worst and probably the
most effective. If Faith wasn't such an angelic, dreamy-
eyed dope, she'd have opened her box and read the letter
right away." Gerry continued forthrightly, "But Faith
being Faith—" Her mouth pursed in thought, and then
she asked, "How do you think she's really reacting to the
idea of Pat's return?"

"Well, if I figure it rightly she's happy and excited, and
yet she's sort of frightened. Shy—" Cathy paused, studying Gerry across the small table in the crowded room with
its babble of lunchers, marveling again at the contrast
between Gerry, with her vivid, outgoing ways, her air of
being born for exhilaration, and Faith, the symbol of all

that was somehow sad and sweet and ethereal. "It was almost as though she was relieved when she heard he wouldn't be home for another week."

Cathy paused again, her eye registering color pleasure while the waitress set individual pink casseroles of golden cheese soufflé on the green place mats in front of them, pink plates of fresh pineapple salad, pots of tea and a pink lacquered basket of crusty French bread. "That's what puzzles me, Gerry. I feel that way about Rex, too." Then at last she was telling Gerry about her phone call and the thrilling prospect of getting started on her dance with Rex's sister Rachel. Gerry's interest and enthusiasm were as gratifyingly complete as Cathy had anticipated. "Well, what I mean about Faith," she concluded, switching back to that part of the conversation, "is that I never knew you'd feel shy the way she does at twenty-six."

Gerry smiled understandingly. "You thought getting married maybe automatically made you wise and self-confident?"

"Something like that."

"If I didn't adore Faith so, I could shake her. She's the most ineffectual person." Gerry sighed. "The only impulsive thing Faith has ever done was to marry Pat. It might have helped—it still might—if she weren't so waited on hand and foot, if she just had to get out and dig."

"Bettina said something this morning that startled me," Cathy confided. "She said I was like Faith." She made a little face, recalling the queer, curiously chilled feeling she had had at the comparison. "Just as well, I guess, that I've had to buckle down and look after the kids. And now, with all this dance practice I'll have to squeeze in, well, I won't have a second to spare. It's just these two weeks at Faith's that are so strange with nothing special to do."

"Oh, everyone needs a breather for dreaming now and then. And I must say it's wonderful to see you turning your thoughts out beyond your circle at home."

Quite unaware of the seriousness of her tone, Cathy asked, leaning forward, "Did you—I mean, have you— daydreamed a lot about one certain person?"

"Like mad," Gerry assured her honestly.

"There's always someone fiercely in love with you, Gerry," Cathy said with a smile.

"But the one special person hasn't come along. And, anyway, right now I'm pretty well wrapped up in my career. As for you, darling, just work away on your career, too."

"You're trying to say don't count on Rex, aren't you?"

Surprisingly, Gerry answered the question by asking one of her own. "Haven't you ever daydreamed about Walt?"

"Glory, no!" Cathy's unconscious vehemence spoke her scornful amusement at the very idea. "Oh, I've worried about his inventions. Honestly, I've been almost ashamed about the way I can spot a flaw."

"Maybe that's just being practical."

"Like his de-fleaing dog bed—" She sighed and buttered a last piece of French bread. "It had a vacuum business in it, you know, and of course it's just dandy on a Boston bull, or a dachshund, or any short-haired dog. But you take a woolly mat like Jimbo, and any little flea is perfectly safe and cozy."

Gerry said, "But a lot of those things he hatched out while he was pretty kiddish. Now his carburetor—not that I know anything about it—but I do know he's got a brain that's clicking all the time, and one of these days that extra measure of steam is going to hit the jackpot. Besides, he's mighty nice and mighty good looking. I

should think there'd be a lot of girls at school who'd find
him just about right."

"Oh, sure," Cathy said absently. "I've seen girls stop
him in the halls to chat." Now that she tried to remember who they were and what they individually looked
like, they all merged into the prancing figure of the sopho-
more cheer leader in her short pleated skirt and high
boots. Idly now she wondered whether Walt had really
liked her.

"Maybe they think you're lucky to have someone like
Walt always around, always there when you need an
escort."

"That's funny," Cathy confided. "You know, I never felt
I rated at school when the girls talked dates." How could
you feel romantic about a boy who rubbed it in about
your signing up for folk dancing just so you could get out
of hockey; who didn't believe you had any real talent for
a ballet career; whose "We'll see" booming in her thoughts
still held a taunt even though he may not have meant it
that way? Aloud she said, "Golly, Gerry, Walt knows
everything about me. He even claims he sucked a honey
bee stinger out of my heel when I was only four, only I
don't remember it; and I really doubt that it happened,
because he would only have been five and a half."

"Hey, don't get yourself so worked up." Gerry's good-
natured laugh was so infectious that it brought a blush
to Cathy's face, and then abruptly she was laughing lightheartedly herself. That was what was so wonderful about
Gerry—just being with her had a way of making life fun.

Gerry regarded Cathy over the rim of her teacup.
"Anyway, I'm absolutely delighted that you've run into
such luck with Rex's sister, and I hope all your dreams of
dancing with Rex and eventually becoming professional
come true."

"If I could just convince Dad that I need the very best teacher possible! That class I was in was just baby stuff."

Gerry waved this difficulty away and reached across to pat Cathy's hand. "We'll all gang up and put in a pitch for you."

Secretly Cathy was not at all sure that this would help. She didn't know exactly how swayed her father would be by Gerry's exuberance. His remote hospital world was practically another planet. "If he does spend the money on my ballet lessons there goes the second-hand car he promised me for my seventeenth birthday. With six of us at home, there's always someone going somewhere."

"Well, you'll have to choose." Gerry sobered. "Making a choice against obstacles is always part of realizing an ambition. It takes courage."

Under Gerry's very nice, straight little nose and generous, quick-smiling mouth there was a square and determined jaw, unobtrusive and softened by her ready sympathy, her gaiety, but there. Now Gerry's level gaze seemed to be measuring her very spirit, Cathy thought, and suddenly memory took her back to Walt. Walt had looked at her the same way out on the hillside when they had quarreled.

Cathy groaned. "But when you've got three young sisters and two brothers all counting the days, thrilled to the bone over your birthday for the simple reason that it means a car for them all to go places in—" Now the full impact of the appalling and unaccustomed prospect of denying her family a longed-for treat in favor of something strictly for herself struck her. Her heart seemed a stone. A mouthful of pecan pie refused to go down. The warmth of the attractive little restaurant had evaporated, the hum of cozy chatter and the mingled fragrance of perfume and food that had enfolded her a moment ago seemed to have receded.

"Well, you don't have to decide this instant," Gerry mused aloud. "This is pure wishful thinking, Cathy, and I wouldn't count on it, but there's Bettina's idea that Pat is bringing each of us a sackful of diamonds." She smiled. "If he could bring us each just one diamond now—"

Cathy shrugged, valiantly rallying to Gerry's banter. "Which reminds me, Betts is simply soaked to her ears in mystery. You know there was someone hiding in the shrubbery, and Betts has a theory that it's someone who knows Pat is returning and that he might actually have some diamonds with him."

"Possible, but not very probable." Gerry's dark brows puckered. "I've been wondering myself who could have been out there. It's baffling." She thought some more. "I wonder whether Pat is really back in this country. Oh, it's tantalizing to have to clock the days until next week. And here you are," she concluded with a glance that drew Cathy into the circle of her thoughts, "doing the same thing about Rex. Waiting a week for his return."

"But how about the Paris hat? It's obviously an imported hat, really dreamy, but it came from a shop here in San Francisco. Do you suppose he wrote to the shop? Or did he actually pick it out in town himself?"

"But if he did that," Gerry continued this line of reasoning, "why doesn't he come home right away? Why? Why? Why?"

"The hat's so exactly right for Faith that he must have chosen it." All at once giggles broke through Cathy's thinking. "Can you imagine Dad picking out a hat? Or Rick? Or Walt?" The giggles subsided to glowing confidence again. "Rex could, though. He's the Paris hat type."

The glow was mirrored in Gerry's face, conveying her understanding. "I know what you mean. It takes a special kind of imagination and sensitivity, and yet—" She paused, admonishment mingling with flippancy. "Don't forget, my lamb, the Paris hat type can break your heart, too." Then suddenly she was scrabbling her things together, the check, her bag and gloves, a portfolio she had to drop at another office. "I've got to run now. Don't forget, you're coming over with Walt to try prumond recipes Sunday night."

Cathy found herself smiling again. "I just happened to think—Walt's the big striped bass type. Remember how tickled he was when he brought me one yesterday?"

Gerry gave her an odd look. "Don't sell Walt short, Cathy. Even a big striped bass could be sprinkled with stardust for many a gal."

It wasn't until Cathy was home that she remembered she had not asked Gerry about the mystery of the marshmallow box. Had Gerry told Faith about the note in the box?

8

Russian Hill Rendezvous

GERRY'S APARTMENT WAS close to the bay on one
of Russian Hill's steepest but most picturesquely winding
streets. The forty-eight steps that Grandma had complained about had to be climbed to the building entrance.
Once inside, you took an elevator to the top floor, where
Gerry's apartment, with its great glassed-in living room
gave an impression of being airborne. The view from the
kitchen at night showed the great bridges nearby, with
their twinkling lights, the black expanse of water, and the
dark mysterious hulks of ships lined up along the shadowed Embarcadero.

Inside, the *décor* was what Gerry laughingly labeled
"antique modern." She had painted the kitchen a persimmon red, with brown cupboard doors. Rows of copper-
bottomed pans hung around a copper-hooded stove. She
had high, white, starched chef's hats for Walt and Rick
and white chef's aprons for everyone. In her brown velvet

104

toreador pants and persimmon sweater Gerry looked like one of her own fashion ads, designed to go with the kitchen.

Only Rick protested with exaggerated groans. "No apron for me! I only volunteered to taste."

Bettina, because she was self-appointed custodian of the cookbook, took over as self-appointed chairman. Imperiously she rapped for attention with a ladle. "We're here to test suitable recipes to use Walt's prumonds so that he can present them in their most delicious forms to the public."

"Hear! Hear!" Walt put in, producing a great sack of prune-pit kernels.

Gerry opened a cookbook. "I vote we try marzipan."

Rick cupped a hand behind his ear. "Marzi—what?"

"Ground almonds to you—made into a perfectly heavenly candy that's horribly expensive. It'll use up a lot of prumonds, too, because you start right off with—" Here she started to read. "One pound of almonds ground at least four times."

"I'll do the grinding," Walt volunteered. "Lead on to the grinder, Cathy."

"When we're through with the marzipan, we'll make prumond macaroons, prumond toffee, and prumond apricot conserve," Bettina supplemented, "and then if we have any time left we can try orange-prumond tarts, chocolate-prumond clusters—"

"Hold on," Gerry advised. "One thing at a time. Or, on second thought, since there are five of us here, maybe we could do two things at a time."

"We'll work in teams: Cathy and Walt and Rick and I," Bettina outlined. "And Gerry can boss because she's too beautiful in her brown velvet pants to cook."

"I look beautiful in my gray flannels," Rick insisted,

"so I'll stay right here and decorate the davenport. Oh,
I'll open my mouth from time to time for tidbits you
want tested."

With a humorous sigh Bettina assumed Grandma's inflection. "How can anyone be so lazy?"

Cathy found herself presiding over a series of mixing
bowls and a kettle of bubbly chocolate while Walt measured ingredients. Eventually Rick was pressed into but-
tering some pans, although he claimed it was involuntary
servitude.

Cathy had planned a little apology to Walt, but in the
crowded kitchen, with Gerry's and Bettina's good-natured
banter flowing over everything, there wasn't a suitable
moment. She was thankful to see that any awkwardness
she had felt over her quarrel with Walt wasn't reflected
in him. He was just the same as always, honest, rugged,
with an air of easy, pliant confidence that seemed to say,
"If this doesn't work, something else will." At that very
moment, as though reading her thoughts, Walt remarked,
"These are kind of small and maybe not exactly as tasty
as almonds." He paused, stuffing a handful of kernels into
the grinder. "But nothing ventured, nothing gained."

As always, Cathy found herself falling into the familiar
pattern of admiration for the unbeatable quality that
turned his inventiveness around another corner when the
last one had led to a blank wall. She wished she had
only a quarter of his self-assurance to bolster her resolve
to be a dancer. She had vowed to show him that she
could be a good professional dancer. But what if she
failed? What if she couldn't make the grade?

Then all thought of herself was banished when she
heard Bettina ask Gerry, "Is this a chicken pox or a measle
coming out on my arm?"

"Measle?" Alarm sharpened Cathy's voice.

"I didn't mention it before because I knew you'd have seven kinds of conniptions, but the twins I was visiting with Cora were breaking out with either measles or chicken pox."

"And you stayed there?" Cathy pounced on her.

"Well, the twins were napping, and Bessie didn't notice until they woke up. She was giving herself a home permanent, and I was rolling up her back hair, and then Cora said as long as I'd breathed in measles for that long I was probably saturated with germs, anyway, and I might as well stay for the whole afternoon."

Cathy's brow furrowed in anxiety. "Dad's away at that medical convention—"

"So that's why your house is so quiet. Golly, it's been lonesome over there without even Mee Chow shaking a mop out the back door," Walt told her.

Bettina said, "Dad gave Mee Chow a holiday while we are all away. You know he's got a pack of relatives in Chinatown, but he hardly ever sees them because he says a day off gets him all tired out worrying about us."

"Your father ought to get a good solid woman housekeeper to take his place," Gerry put in.

"But do they make any woman solid enough for those six kids?" Rick's puckish wink took the sting out of his words.

"We're not that hard to take," Bettina bantered. "It's just the number of us that's overwhelming."

"Not to mention that lethal litter of skates and baseballs on your front porch," Rick added.

"Anyway," Bettina admitted, "I guess Mee Chow's the only cook in the world who'd stand for a jar of frog spawn in his refrigerator."

"What?" Cathy spluttered. "That's one they put over on me," she explained apologetically.

"That's what I mean." Gerry shuddered.

"But the outside of the bottle was perfectly clean," Bettina defended. "And the twins wanted to have the spawn so they could have some fresh-hatched tadpoles for Tess's birthday."

Gerry and Rick exchanged a look, and Gerry said, "There's a beguiling thought."

"Well, what's wrong with that?" Rick asked. "Any half-wit knows a few fresh-hatched tadpoles make the ideal birthday present."

Delayed shock gripped Cathy—shock at hearing Gerry, so intuitively understanding, so lightheartedly tolerant, strike at the very backbone of their existence. Just the thought of home without Mee Chow made Cathy feel unstable and as fly-away as an empty paper sack in the wind. All at once the old saying that everyone has a blind spot took on a new meaning. Still, it was hard to believe that Gerry could have a blind spot where their beloved Mee Chow was concerned.

True, there were skates sometimes on the front porch, and episodes like frog spawn in the refrigerator did occur, but with six children in the house what could you expect? For several years now she and Bettina had taken over the morning bedmaking and evening dishwashing, and she, Cathy, had hurried home from school on Tuesdays to help with the endless ironing. But still, the task of housekeeping was tremendous. And it wasn't just housekeeping. It was as though Mee Chow's small, seamed, yellow face, his short, thin, scurrying legs in their flapping cotton trousers, his narrow, nimble, work-worn hands filled every room with warmth and a constant comforting reminder of the daily routine their mother had established years ago. She must make Gerry see—understand. But when she opened her mouth to speak, there were no words adequate for the emotion she felt.

And then right behind her, shoulder against hers, there was Walt filling in her mute need. "Golly, Gerry," he was saying, "you've got Mee Chow all wrong. Why, I bet he does the work of three people twice his size. If you could be there for a whole day sometime—"

That was it, Cathy thought. Gerry was always popping in and out. Actually she couldn't remember when Gerry had spent a whole day in their house.

"Just washing and cooking and cleaning for eight people is no cinch," Walt went on, "not to mention the way he fills in as plumber, gardener, and general handyman."

"Or," Bettina added, "the way he just fixed a lot of my outgrown summer dresses for Fran and some of Fran's for Tess. And he's teaching Cathy to use the sewing machine now so she can do all that, if she has time when she isn't practicing ballet," she tacked on doubtfully.

Cathy's breath caught. *If* I have time! What an *if!*

As though the conversation had taken too serious a turn, Gerry conceded that her remark about Mee Chow had been out of order. "I take back all my harsh words. I see Mee Chow's really a treasure—bless his old heart." Her hand outstretched in a quick gesture begged apology, and then as quickly she turned to Bettina. "And now to change the subject," she offered, "maybe this is just a hive on Bett's arm."

"I hope so," Cathy added fervently. "I'd hate to bother Dad with the chicken pox or measles right now when he's enjoying a little vacation or give it to Faith when she's expecting Uncle Pat home."

"Perish the thought!" Gerry added, just as appalled.

"Well, you can all relax," Bettina assured them, "because I think this red spot's a syrup burn. It splashed when I was testing for a soft ball in cold water. Hey! This is ready now." She lifted a kettle from the stove, and as the room was filled with the noisy whirr of the electric beater going into action, Cathy went out to the service porch to hang up some damp tea towels.

She lingered in the dark at the open window, taking a deep breath, fresh, cool, and welcome after the concentrated sweet, syrupy, chocolaty scents. An eerie kind of moonlight made a luminous, pearly glow of the fog over the Golden Gate. A passing ship sent out a farewell whistle.

In the kitchen someone turned off the electric beater, and Gerry said, "You know, this is really exciting; we should all feel highly honored to be in on the birth of a new food product."

Through the open door Cathy saw Walt's surprised and gratified grin. "To tell the truth, that's the way I've been feeling. Only I didn't expect anyone else to feel exactly the same way. It's such a simple thing—prune pits. And just to stumble on them by accident—well, it almost seems too good to be true. As though someone else should have tried it."

Gerry's head bent appraisingly over the candy-thermometer in the kettle she was watching. "But the world's full of surprises right in front of us if we could only see them."

Walt said, "I was thinking of those scientists who are working now to make food out of plankton. Plankton's microscopic marine life," he explained in answer to Bettina's question. "All they have to do is find a way to gather it in quantities. And then there's algae, another form of highly nutritious marine growth, that might some day be used for commercial cattle feed. When you consider the possibilities and the world need for food—"

Cathy sensed him groping for a word tremendous enough to express the limitless emotion he was experiencing. As she watched him, the word noble popped into her mind. It was odd to think of a boy with a cream-colored crew cut and a sturdy, tanned neck as noble. "It's the kind of nobility one sees in a Great Dane," she thought, both amused and stirred by her simile. If Walt was a Great Dane, what was Rex? Heart abruptly thumping, she tried to think of an animal that would express Rex's eloquence of motion, his compelling quality.

"It's a lovely night for daydreaming," Gerry said, suddenly appearing beside her, "but come back and join the tasters. Our marzipan's a knockout."

With a start Cathy realized that she had been daydreaming, and for some time, too, if the marzipan was finished. "But the strange thing is that at the same time I've been feeling wider awake than ever before. I almost feel as if I've been living a whole new life since seeing the children off to camp." How would she ever settle down to the old routine?

Gerry's mouth had its gentle quirk. "You're growing up. That means a new awareness of everything. I have the same feeling myself often."

"But you're twenty-five. You're grown up."

Gerry laughed. "Not by a long way, I'm afraid."

Walt appeared in the doorway. "What is this—you two —a private conference?"

Gerry shook her head. With her arm around Cathy's waist, she drew her back to the kitchen as Bettina announced firmly, in what was obviously caution to herself, "Now, if we don't quit sampling these things, there won't be any left for Walt to pass around to people who might buy prumonds."

"To say nothing of what it'll do to our waistlines," Gerry added, patting her very slim midriff.

Rick helped himself to a chocolate prumond cluster. "Since I have no waistline to consider and no football training to break—" He chewed silently a moment and then went on. "Which reminds me, I was reading the other day about a tribe of Australian aborigines. Just as our young hunks of football muscle are forbidden tobacco, alcohol, and rich morsels like these, the young braves over there are on their honor to refrain from snakes, turtles, kangaroos, and emu eggs." He fixed Walt with his whimsical gaze. "Remember that next fall when football training clamps down."

"I'll do that." Walt waved a plate of the perfect marzipan overhead with a flourish. "To the lowly prune!"

"May it help make you wealthy!" Gerry followed up exultantly.

Bettina suggested a Walt Special: A prumond macaroon with a marzipan center crowned with a chocolate prumond cluster.

Gerry reeled from the horror of such a suggestion. "Please, please!" she begged. "And please keep your feet out of my philodendrons."

With exaggerated care Rick jack-knifed his lanky legs from their position over the davenport arm and away from the planter box where he'd been resting his feet. "There's no pleasing this woman. You'd think she'd at least want her only brother to be comfortable. There's something grim about women and me," he continued, grinning amiably. "Take Grandma, for instance. She can lie in bed all day, reading her head off. Yet let me settle my bones for one minute on the sofa, and she fixes me with a baleful eye that says I'm a sluggard."

Gerry said, "I've been thinking that perhaps my only brother might like to move in here with me. It might be the answer to your problem."

"I've got a problem?" Rick inquired.

"Well, there's the possibility that you'd like to get out of Grandma's hair."

Rick considered her through the lazy slit of his eyes. "There's the possibility, too," he announced at last, when he could speak again after dropping a whole prumond macaroon into his mouth like a banqueting Roman, "that I might be moving from Grandma's gray mane to your handsome horse tail. To be more specific, while I'm in Grandma's clutches, she'll keep my nose to the grindstone at the bank; but if I'm living with you, my beautiful slave driver, you'll harry me to go back to college."

"What's wrong with college?" Walt burst in reasonably. "My gosh! Here I am breaking my neck to get a chance at it. In fact, I've got to."

"Oh, it's fine for you with your particular type of brain," Rick admitted cheerfully.

"It's fine for anyone," Gerry stated, pushing home her advantage.

"Are you going to college, Cathy?" Rick inquired.

From her place at a card table where she and Walt were packing marzipan in the little aluminum-foil-lined boxes Gerry had provided, Cathy said, "N-o-o-o. I don't need to."

"She's going to be a ballet dancer," Bettina explained for her. "If you're going to be a dancer, you can't waste time educating your brain, because by the time you've put in four years at college your feet are too old. Cathy's feet are almost too old right now, 'cause most ballet dancers start when they're just about able to walk."

That takes care of me, Cathy thought, with a deflating drop of spirit. Then her sense of humor returned. You couldn't really be long out of sorts with Bettina's bubbling candidness. All the same, she was grateful when Bettina turned the talk back to Rick. "Rick, you might be just a borderline case of laziness."

Rick seemed to be considering this obviously true statement. "Thanks for the delicate choice of adjective."

"What beats me is how anyone who hates action like you," Bettina pursued impishly, "can be so crazy about fast things like horses."

"That, my dear young cousin, is because I'm an enigma."

"If you were only Chinese," Bettina told him, "this might be your best year. Your very own year."

Rick's expression registered the courtesy of amused interest. "How does that figure?"

"Remember when we went to the Chinese festival in Chinatown with Mee Chow?" Bettina appealed to Cathy and Walt and then rushed on, carried away by eager reminiscence. "Well, they had their ceremonial dragon —it takes fifty men to make him dance down the street— and thousands of firecrackers going off, and Sze Tze, I think his name is, the wild-eyed lion—he's not a real live lion, of course, but just a terrific costume with men inside —and then they had Chinese sword dancers, and the weirdest kind of sing-song music played on moon harps and things—" Bettina had to pause for breath.

Rick waggled a finger at her. "Hold on. How, may I ask, does all this tie in with my particular fortune?"

Bettina looked blank. Enthusiasm for the remembered scene had run away with her original idea. "Oh, I know," she said finally, with relief, "because every Chinese year has a name, like last year was the year of the snake, and this one's the year of the horse. And it signifies speed and perseverance and stuff like that."

Behind the thick-lensed glasses there was a half-amused, half-serious expression. "The year of the horse," Rick repeated meditatively. "Could be my year at that, though I must confess I don't feel any urge to speed and perseverance."

"But what are you going to do?" Gerry's charging energy challenged. "You can't go on forever working at a job you hate. Seems to me you might better be preparing yourself for a career of some kind that you really like."

Rick's lower lip puckered in the bony frame of his narrow face, rebellion written there, for all the world reminding Cathy of her five-year-old brother Pipper. Here she'd been thinking of Rick as a grown-up cousin, along with Gerry, but part of him was still just a little boy. Their glances locked, and she was conscious of something baffled there, as though he were full of emotions that he wanted to explain but couldn't. And then, with a gulp that seemed to swallow the passing mood, Rick quoted quixotically:

> You must keep your goal in sight
> Labor toward it day and night
> Then at last arriving there
> You shall be too old to care.

The atmosphere lifted. As a companion piece Gerry quoted:

> Climb high,
> Climb far,
> Your goal the sky
> Your aim the star.

Rick scrunched down on the davenport, wriggling his shoulders against a cushion. "Before this year of the horse passes, Patrick McQueen will be home, and perhaps a heart-to-heart talk will settle a lot of things."

9

Bettina Would Tell

LATER, WHEN ALL the efforts of their prumond experiments were packed and ready for Walt to take home, Gerry asked, "Anyone hungry?"

In spite of their sampling, everyone, particularly Bettina, was. Gerry brought out soft drinks, little chicken and watercress sandwiches, potato chips, and carrot sticks.

While Cathy was thinking how good everything salty and tart was after all the sweets, Bettina went scampering off down her favorite conversational path. "What would you do, Gerry, if Uncle Pat really brings us each a little sack of diamonds?"

"Diamonds may be a gal's best friend," Gerry began, "but I think I'd be tempted to convert mine into cash for a trip around the world. Paris, Vienna, Rome, mostly Paris, Paris in the spring, tra-la, tra-la," she trilled. Hands clasped behind her head, she faced Cathy. "I'd bring you and Betts each a Paris hat, so that Faith wouldn't have a complete corner on the heavenly hat department."

From her perch on the cushioned window seat, hunched knees cradled in her arms, a luxurious sigh came from Bettina. "I'd convert mine into cash, too. I'd buy bedspreads for everyone at home," she said. "Simply lovely ones like Faith has. Only, something we could roll on, too. And then I'd buy Rick a horse—a real Arabian horse, all shiny jet, named Black Prince, that could run like the wind. I'd get Cathy the best ballet teacher in the world, and if there was any money left I'd give it to you, Walt, for college."

Silence fell on the group after this all-inclusive recital of extravagant bounty, broken only when Gerry crossed the room and dropped a kiss on the top of Bettina's head. "My darling, you put me to shame with your generosity. Here I was thinking of myself first."

Walt said, "I guess each of us would have thought of himself first."

Bettina shrugged. "But I got my bicycle last Christmas." With that Bettina shed the accolade, as though already possessing last year's heart's desire took care of everything. "Anyway," she added, scratching her leg with twelve-year-old unconsciousness, "all I hope is that if Uncle Pat is bringing home some diamonds that old diamond thief doesn't get them."

"May I," Rick inquired, "ask what 'old diamond thief'?"

"You know," Bettina explained, "that man who was hiding in the bushes."

In answer to a question from Walt, Gerry said, "I guess we forgot to tell you. There was someone hanging around Faith's house the other night. Faith's neighbor called to tell us."

"And then we found his footprints back of the rhododendrons," Bettina put in. She turned, addressing Rick:

"Did we tell you that while we were examining the footprints the next morning Jimbo brought us his chewing
shoe to try on for size?"

"Did it fit?" Rick asked.

Gerry caught her breath. "Did it?"

"We didn't even try it," Bettina said, "because no dog
could set a shoe down to make exact footprints."

"But if one of Pat's shoes did fit the prints," Gerry went
on, "why, then, it must have been Pat out there."

"But Jimbo's chewing shoe came from the meter reader.
He's had a crush on Cora because she always gives him
coffee and cheese cake or pie or something, so he brought
one of his old shoes as a present for Jimbo."

"But we could still try one of Pat's shoes in the prints,"
Gerry pursued. "There must be some over there at
Faith's."

Cathy shook her head dubiously. "Jimbo rolled on the
prints, so I don't think we could measure exactly."

Gerry sighed. "Well, that squashes that little plan."

Cathy noticed that Walt's mouth was open as though
he was going to say something. Then he closed it, obviously changing his tack. After a moment, with seeming
irrelevance, he said, "I've been meaning to tell you. I
think I've got someone really interested in my new carburetor."

"What?" The old habit of interest in his inventions, so
deeply rooted, jerked the question out of Cathy with eager
delight.

There was a barrage of questions from the group. "You
mean you're going to be rich even if prumonds don't sell
like hot cakes?" Bettina demanded. "And you'll be famous
with your very own carburetor whizzing past us in every
car?"

"Hardly. Nothing's that easy." Walt's flicker of amuse-

ment at Bettina's little-girl simplification slid into soberness. "Even if I get the last bug worked out and it's the
practical gas-saving baby I feel sure it's going to be,
there's still a long road to go."

"Oh, good gravy!" Bettina clapped her hand to her
brow in a typically dramatic Bettina way. "I just happened to think of something—a ghastly movie I saw.
There was this young inventor, sort of a big, handsome,
trusting guy, just like Walt, who had this formula for a
new kind of rubber that would last forever, practically.
And he sold the formula to a sinister gangster kind of guy
who paid him off with just little peanuts and a lot of prom-
ises and then tore up the plans like that," she made an
exaggerated tearing motion, "so they could keep on making their old tires that wear out fast and people would
have to buy more and they could make more money."

"Oh, such a thing couldn't really happen. It wouldn't
be fair." Cathy wasn't conscious of her indignation.

Walt laughed. "Sure it would. As the big, handsome,
trusting type—" he winked at Bettina "—I'm well aware
that big monopolies have done just that time and again."

"But why?" Cathy insisted.

"Sometimes they shelve new inventions just so their ma-
chinery won't be obsolete." He shrugged his square shoulders. There was his undaunted grin. "It's something
you've got to face."

Bettina's furious loyalty spluttered. "But that would be
absolutely skunky."

"Nevertheless, it does happen," Gerry agreed. She
stood in front of the work table that held her paints and
brushes before the big north window. There was the start
of an evening gown fashion sketch on the drawing board,
and beyond her the view of the night was studded with
nubs of light that marked the miracle of the Golden Gate

bridge. A far-off meditativeness reflected in her eyes gave way to inspiration. "You know, Pat might be just the one to advise you. I remember now there was a new drill used in diamond mining—something completely revolutionary—that was at least part of his interest in going to Africa. Someone he knew had invented it."

Bettina jumped up and down, black bangs flapping. "Oh, if Uncle Pat doesn't come home soon, we're all just going to burst! Wouldn't it be wonderful if we waked up tomorrow and found it's the day?" As though her fizz of excitement had all at once consumed her energy, she plumped down on the davenport beside Rick and began to sing.

Suddenly they were all singing favorite old-time songs. Cathy and Bettina had been harmonizing with Walt's sturdy baritone ever since it had turned baritone. Now Gerry's throaty contralto and Rick's tenor added the full complement. Walt's arm pumped in joyous time-keeping.

Under the rich, swelling sound and warmth of friendly happiness, Cathy's thoughts rushed to the rising crescendo of eagerness that was the promise of the trip to Telegraph Hill tomorrow to get acquainted with Rex's sister Rachel, to get started on that dance. For a transient moment Rex's image took possession of her so vividly that when Walt's big hand paused in its time-keeping to clasp hers in a rollicking swing of friendship, Cathy had trouble bringing herself back to reality. She was thankful for the cover-up of Walt's clowning as he turned and grabbed up one of Gerry's paint brushes for a baton. He led them on in noisy abandon in another song. And then, strangely, in the midst of all this, she was startled to think, "What if the shoe were on the other foot? What if Walt had a new interest, a new girl in his life who took up all his thoughts?" There had been so few reservations between

them during all these years that now to have something
in her life that he not only did not share but actually
seemed to distrust and resist was a strange and disturbing
experience, indeed.

The unaccustomed picture stirred her to new confusion,
so that all she could think of was an urgency to apologize
for her hasty, hateful words of the other night. Fortunately, as they were getting ready to leave, Gerry invited
Bettina to spend the night, and Cathy and Walt rode
back alone.

There was the familiar lurch of Walt's jalopy, the
familiar blast of cold night air blowing over her feet
through the crack where the door didn't fit. Ordinarily
their happiest, most sociable time was their homecoming
together. But tonight the silence between them seemed
fraught with heaviness.

Cathy wondered what was the matter with her? She
ought to be able to just say, "Look, I'm sorry I was snap-
pish the other night." And he'd say, "That's O.K., Lefty,"
and that would be that.

But even as she considered, Walt said, "I hear your
dancing partner, Rex, didn't turn up the other night."

Bettina would tell, of course, and with her flair for
dramatizing, heaven knew how she had built it up. "He
couldn't come," she said, annoyed at the way her voice
faltered defensively, giving away the secret letdown that
even now flooded back at the remembrance. "He had to
go out of town. He's dancing in a TV film they're making
in Hollywood." A little of her pride in knowing Rex, of
her thrill of association, returned and was as quickly dis-
pelled when Walt said, "Seems like he could have called
you instead of letting you wonder and wait."

All the friendly urge she had felt to re-establish their
old closeness was suddenly gone. Did Bettina have to tell

everything? Did Walt have to put a finger on the exact sore spot? Why, just a moment ago she would have said that it was impossible for Walt to be nosy or to rub it in if he did find out something humiliating, something smarting. She bit her tongue to hold back the desperate denial that she longed to hurl at him, while waves of disagreeable meaning seemed to ripple out from his words.

Well, let Walt think Rex was handing her a line if he wanted. Certainly that was what he was thinking. They drove on, not speaking. Cathy's lips pressed tight together, and her thoughts pressed tight against any little wisps of doubt that Walt's implied accusation might try to stir again. Back at Faith's she jumped out of the car and ran up the steps without a backward glance. But of course Walt was right behind her. She wasn't going to be able to close the door without speaking some kind of word. "Thanks for the ride." It was all she could manage in her bewildered hurt. Only after the door was closed and she leaned weakly against the banister in the dark, honesty forced admission, "That's funny. He wasn't really exulting at all. He just looked worried."

10

Rachel

CATHY COULDN'T REMEMBER ever having been on Telegraph Hill alone before. She had come there with her father, and long ago she and the children had come kiting with Walt. A winding road led to the peak, where in far-off gold-rush days a semaphore had signaled the coming of sailing ships through the Golden Gate. Now there was Coit Tower, which people climbed in clear weather to enjoy the view of bridges and water, of islands and ships, and the distant dazzle of sunshine on the hills beyond by day and starshine by night.

Cathy's thoughts lingered on the details of the tale that had fascinated them all as children, a tale that said Mrs. Coit's husband, in whose memory she had built the tower, had been renowned solely for his love of chasing fire engines. It may or may not be true, she mused, but she was glad to think of anything that might remotely tickle her funnybone.

124

Back at Faith's it had been all very well to let the fore-stage of her imagination shimmer in a rainbow of foot-lights as she pirouetted with Rex, but here, approaching Rex's house, she was all too wide-awakely aware of her meager technique. Even the hours of daily practice that she had been putting in now seemed scaringly inadequate and full of mistakes.

Her pulse jarred her with its heavy thuds as the house number she sought appeared before her, seeming twice its natural size, long before she was ready. Vaguely her outer eye registered the house as being one of the oldest of a number of small wooden structures squeezed in among modern apartment buildings on three sides, so that the magnificent view it surely must have once had was now hopelessly lost. To Cathy its weathered, wind-blown list matched her own crazily listing insides. As she went up the steps, old, crumbling, and uneven with time and hillside settling, she saw that they had been originally built by a sculptor. For the risers of the steps were inset with small bas reliefs of beautifully modeled sea urchins and starfish; and even the niche for the mail-box was a lichen-covered sculpture of dolphins with tails entwined, almost hidden by a great, gnarled, overhanging pepper tree. A pair of spotted sandpipers, with their familiar peet-weet, peet-weet, swooped down like falling skyrockets to strut on the edge of a dilapidated fountain now filled with earth and overgrown with rank moss verbena and geraniums.

Only by drawing close the cherished words of Rex there on the school stage, only by steadying herself with the far-off rapture of their dance together could she summon courage to raise the old-fashioned knocker, its brass long encrusted by the green verdigris of time and salt sea air.

Cathy knew she would have recognized the girl who opened the door as Rex's sister had she met her anywhere. Rachel had the feminine counterpart of Rex's sleekness, burnished dark, the same odd slanting eyes, a high cheek-boned narrow face, which in her made for piquancy rather than prettiness. But even in their first moment of meeting, in Cathy's fumbling introduction, the eyes that regarded her under the dark, straight brows were remotely preoccupied. She's worried, Cathy thought with quick intuition, worried and sort of listening for something.

Rachel was in practice dress, a simple, black-ribbed leotard that revealed and accentuated the firmness of her lean figure, the assured regal grace of motion. Her smooth black hair was caught tight in the ballerina's traditional chignon.

Rachel said, "I was about to do some practicing myself, so we can work together." She showed Cathy where to hang her things, and as Cathy bent to tie on her ballet slippers, she noticed that their living room was obviously their practice room, too. The floor's dark varnish was scuffed, worn-looking. She saw an old square piano, with the score for *Les Sylphides* on the rack, and, to one side, a record player. Along one side wall there was a practice *barre* and on the opposite a broad, full-length mirror.

Cathy judged Rachel to be a year or two older than Rex, which would make her nineteen or twenty. They had warmed up at the *barre* for only a few minutes when Rachel paused in her own exercise to come to Cathy's side. "Here," she said, tapping a knee, "this must be straighter." Her aloof preoccupation disappeared, and she was all authority, her attention appraising, concentrated. Her hands, slender, strong, and supple, moved along Cathy's back to straighten it, lightly pressed the shoulder blades down, the chin up, and adjusted her

balance so that her weight was forward, distributed
evenly on the balls of her feet, her heels barely resting
on the floor. After another period at the *barre*, Rachel
called Cathy away for center work, indicating the steps
and clapping her hands to emphasize the beat of time,
and then with a quick gesture she broke the action while
Cathy stood with hands and brow icy, hair clinging to
her damp neck, muscles quivering with exertion and
nervousness. Finally Rachel signaled for Cathy to rest.

Leaning gratefully against the wall, Cathy heard her
own gasping breath whistle through the room, and then
all was drowned in music as Rachel placed the needle on
a record. Cathy, unprepared, gasped again, overcome
with utter, breathless wonder, the beauty of Rachel's
motions, one flowing into the other, almost too beautiful
to bear. Her fleet, incisive turns, her spin of effortless
fouettés, her prolonged, steady *arabesques* released with
such delicate, precise timing were a glimpse into enchantment. The same enchantment she had glimpsed when
Rex danced.

The words of Cathy's former dancing teacher came
back. "At first you must sense and feel each muscle;
suffer, too; and then finally you are able to forget everything, all technique, and lose yourself in your own style."
Had Rachel, this lovely floating gossamer Rachel,
suffered? Cathy's slender shoulders squared. A longing
to work, work, work seized her. She would work until
she, too, could dance such sheer excitement. For an
instant it all seemed quite possible, the only desirable
thing in life. "I can do it," she told herself. Then im-
mediately, swiftly, there was the humble, bottom-falling-
out-of-the-world feeling.

"Oh, I'll never be able to dance like that," she burst out
in desolation.

Rachel paused in front of her, putting her hands weightlessly on Cathy's shoulders. "But you are just starting." Kindness spoke from the dark eyes under the thick lashes. "You know a good many of the fundamental ballet steps—yes. But you know them with your mind only. You do not yet know them with your heart. You cannot expect—"

"But I've had two years of lessons," Cathy admitted honestly, "and this year of folk dancing at school."

"And I," Rachel told her, "have had ten years of study, ten years of daily practice of never less than two hours—sometimes four and five." A shadow of sadness passed over her expressive face. "Two years ago I was ready for professional engagements." She seemed now to be talking almost to herself, inner turbulence tumbling out with the words. "But I fell in love. I was bewitched." Her fingers twisted the wide gold wedding band on her left hand.

"Are you sorry?"

Rachel sighed. "Not really. It's just hard. I get impatient with Rod away in the service." A cry from somewhere in the back of the house broke the stillness between them. Darting off, Rachel said, "That's Bruce, my baby." So this was what Rachel had been listening for. "Come into the kitchen. I've got to heat his milk," she called back.

Following the sound of Rachel's voice, Cathy went down the hall and into a small, old-fashioned kitchen. Between squalls, the baby's narrow face over his mother's shoulder held a smaller scale of Rachel's appeal—and Rex's, too. Everything that was maternal in Cathy seemed to fold around it, including the tiny, jerky arms stiff with anger, the bare, narrow, kicking feet, the thin legs faintly bluish under the pink brunette skin.

Settling herself on a kitchen chair, Rachel tried to insert the nipple in the open circle of the baby's protesting mouth, only to have it spat out. "Now, Brucie, here's your milk. Here's your nice bottle." But tense anxiety belied the crooning words.

Watching, Cathy got the impression of a tug-of-war between these two, anxiety turning to fierce determination, determination settling down to despair. A little dew of perspiration glinted on Rachel's upper lip. She changed arms, shifting the shrilling baby to the other side and offering the bottle with her other hand.

"This is the way it is half the time. He's hungry but he just won't eat." She spoke between the squalls of strident sound, appallingly loud to be coming from such a tiny frame. "I don't know—" She tried again. "I sometimes wonder if he's allergic to milk, or—" She paused, swiveling around on the chair to set the bottle on the table. "Or maybe he's just allergic to me." And then, as though to make up for the implication of her words, the girl leaned forward and kissed the tiny, waving foot in adoring contrition. "He's got a dancer's feet. Oh, you'll be a dancer, yes, you will," she said in soft, hopeful pride as she lifted the baby and touched his forehead to hers. "Rod, the baby's father, is a dancer. He's with an entertainment unit overseas." The ringing phone brought Rachel to her feet. "Here—"

Cathy found herself holding Bruce, found herself straining shamelessly as Rachel's answering voice at the phone in the hall cried, "Oh, Rex. Yes—how's it going?"

Automatically Cathy's arms cradled the baby, one hand reaching for the bottle. She hardly noticed when he took it and began to suck with contentment. Ears still registering acutely, she gleaned only disappointment from Rachel's end of the conversation followed by her

despairing assurance that she could *not* do something
Rex was obviously urging her to do; and underlying all
was haste, the breaking mid-sentence that accompanies a
long-distance call in a house where pennies matter desper-
ately.

When Rachel returned, the oval of Cathy's face was
bent over a peacefully feeding baby, one hand supporting
the bottle, the other moving in gentle massage on the
relaxed infant's back.

"Why, he's eating like a lamb," Rachel breathed. "My
goodness!"

Cathy looked up, quite surprised at the outburst.
"Sure," she said casually. "He's hungry."

Rachel hovered over the sight with brooding eyes.
"But a minute ago he was as stubborn as—Well, how did
you do it? I guess you're used to children?"

Aware of the implied praise, but not especially grateful, Cathy replied, "I should be; I'm the oldest of six."
With a practiced motion she put the baby up to her
shoulder, patting him lightly. Absently she began to
hum under her breath a soft, wordless lullaby, her cheek
pressed against the small silky head.

"Babies know," Rachel said. "It's funny how they
know." Her wistfulness touched Cathy. "He knows I'm
impatient. He knows it just by instinct, I guess." She
turned with a gesture of impotence. "I want him to grow
up fast so he can dance, so we can share dancing—"
She broke off with something like embarrassment. "I
know that sounds silly. I just had no idea babies could
be so—so demanding." She sat down in front of Cathy
again. Cathy sensed a return of the abstraction that had
been so apparent in Rachel earlier. "If I could only stop
being a mother for just a week. Or maybe for just three
days."

Easing the baby back to his bottle, Cathy asked, "Why? I mean, is there some special reason?"

"Things aren't going well for Rex in Hollywood. The partner they've assigned to him isn't right. She's almost deliberately not right. It's hard to explain, but I know what he means, and he's terribly depressed—almost ready to give up the whole thing. He wants me to fly down right away, tonight."

"But don't you have someone who'd keep Bruce for you? Your mother?" Cathy queried.

"Oh, mother—" There was unconscious supplication, longing, in the cry. Then in a moment she went on quite matter-of-factly, "My mother thought I was throwing myself and my career away when I married Rod, so she figures that what happens to me now is my own problem." She got up and began to pace. Then, raising her arms, she turned slowly on point with the utmost floating grace. "Did you ever catch sunlight in your palm?" There was nothing about the words that invited answer. "I have. And I've felt moonlight in my throat. And I've had fire touch me, too. That's dancing with Rex."

"That's dancing with Rex," Cathy's heart echoed. "I've been touched with the same fire," she wanted to say, "just for a moment, maybe, and in a small way compared with you, Rachel. But I know. I know." She knew now, too, the limitations of herself as a dancer, but she understood. And watching Rachel turn again with a melting motion of illuminating beauty, she knew that Rachel must join Rex. Their work together must be put on film for all to enjoy.

"I could take care of Bruce." The spontaneity of her offer surprised Cathy herself, the words bubbling out with such complete lack of premeditation that she felt for an instant as though she couldn't be hearing her own voice.

Something of the same emotion seemed to affect Rachel. She paused, speechless, and then said, "You could? You would?" The emphasis in her repetition held hope and tremulous, excited interest. Swiftly she knelt in front of the baby in Cathy's lap. "I've known you only an hour, but I'd trust him with you. I really would."

A gusty sigh escaped Cathy. "I know. I've got that look." Her sense of humor wanted to spill over in a shaky laugh, but she saw that there were tears brimming in Rachel's eyes, and she busied herself with the bottle until Rachel could brush the tears away.

"But your mother—" Rachel questioned at last. "Won't she mind?"

"Mother died three years ago. Pipper was only two."

"Oh." Rachel touched her, a touch that communicated unspoken comfort. "No wonder you're so adept. You've been—"

"A busy little bee," Cathy filled in. "Only we have Mee Chow, of course, who's what everyone says is the last of the old-time Chinese cooks and housekeepers. His father worked for my grandfather when he first came to San Francisco from China as a boy. Now Mee Chow has worked for us ever since before I was born, and our big family drives him crazy, but he's crazy about us, too. And I guess we love him more than anyone else in the world next to Dad." Then hastily qualifying this statement, she tacked on, "Next to Dad and our very own folks, like Grandma and our special cousins, like Gerry and Rick, and Faith, who's an aunt, but terribly young. And our favorite Uncle Pat, who's coming home any day now after being away for a long, long time."

"But how about your father? Will he mind your having Bruce?"

When the last explanation had been made, and the last of Rachel's doubts had vanished, Cathy felt herself caught up in the other girl's whirl of excitement and activity.

"There's an hour's ride to the airport, but I can make that six o'clock plane. I'll wire Rex right away. I can get in three or four hours' rehearsal with him tonight. The baby's formula is pasted on the ice box door—clean diapers and shirts on the line. Oh, I wish I hadn't skipped washing everything this morning." Dresser drawers flipped in and out; Rachel's hands flew from the meager contents of her closet to her scuffed suitcase, every motion synchronized with grace. "You'll have to use shopping bags for the bottles and things. They're hanging on the kitchen door. His cod liver oil's in the bathroom. And, oh, I'm afraid he's a dreadfully early waker. There isn't a wink of sleep in him after five. You're sure, now, sure it will be all right with your Aunt Faith?" The question was purely rhetorical. There couldn't be any backing out now, with Rachel's suitcase packed, coat laid out on the bed, and Rachel herself zipping up her one good black dress. The clipped instructions, injunctions, and apologies went on in a torrent while Cathy followed about, Bruce cradled expertly on one arm, while with the other she helped, checked, and investigated according to instructions.

Finally packed and ready to go, Rachel stopped the dynamo of speech and action to look at Bruce, every expressive line of her dancer's body momentarily straining toward the brightly watchful, but now contented, child. Lifting him from Cathy's arms, she held him close for a moment. "If I just don't fly out of here this instant, I won't be able to go at all," she whispered, handing him back.

"I'll take good care of him," Cathy reassured. "You don't need to worry."

Rachel's gaze met Cathy's, held intently. "I know you will. And I'll make it up to you." A little smile touched her lips. "You want to dance with Rex, don't you?"

"Yes." The answer was that simple, that direct.

"You'll dance with him," Rachel promised. "You'll dance very nicely, too. I'll help you. I'll see that you have lessons."

Delight and glory welled in Cathy. The very unexpectedness of Rachel's words sent faith in her chosen future as a dancer flooding back.

Rachel opened her purse, handed out the key. "Leave it under the tails of the dolphins at the mail box. I should give you money for a taxi. . . ." She started to count it out.

"Oh, no. I won't need it." Cathy's troubled eyes saw the meager sum in the girl's hand, and her mind rushed ahead, practically figuring plane fare, hotel, meals. "I'll manage. I have a friend who'll come to get us."

As Cathy turned back to the quiet house, Rachel's hurrying footsteps echoed thinly down the outside walk. Walt! She didn't dare call Walt. He'd say gloatingly, "You see. What did I tell you? If that's the way you're made, if you're cut out to be a mother hen, well—" No, she didn't want Walt even to know about Bruce. Now alone, faced with her responsibility, the impulsiveness of what she had done caught up with her.

11

Entrechat Dix

CATHY'S OFFER HAD SEEMED perfectly reasonable while Rachel was with her, while she had been enthralled by the spell of Rachel's dancing. But now, mind leaping ahead, she had a sober picture of herself entering Faith's house with a strange infant, bags of bottles and diapers, cod liver oil, tinned milk. And what an ironic turn of fate that she would soon be using Faith's basement laundry room to do up Rex's nephew's diapers when she had once planned to dance there with Rex! Oh, if she only had Gerry's wonderful self-confidence, her ability to turn a daring deed into light-hearted caprice, acceptable, understandable.

Now she realized that she didn't even know what day Rachel would return to claim her child. And there was her incredible oversight in neglecting to get the name of a hotel or other Hollywood address where she could reach Rachel. Bruce moved in the circle of her arm,

135

gurgled, gave her a soft baby-fist blow on the chin as he stretched. With a further backwash of dismay she realized that she didn't even know his last name or how old he was.

Feeling almost unreal, her worries subsiding, she was suddenly mindful that for this brief time before she left, she was free to give herself to the atmosphere of this house, which was dedicated to ballet and its practitioners. One hand reached down to set the needle on Rachel's record. She moved dreamily with the music, turned with Bruce to observe their reflection from every angle in the full-length mirror. There was something almost mesmeric about the motion of her own rippling hair against her shoulders, the reflection of gray eyes in the silver depths of the mirror. She posed as though in dance, turned again to observe the miniature perfection of Bruce's bright sprite's face, the small mirrored delicacy of his feet. Lifting her gaze, she picked up the reflection of the window opposite, through which she saw low, white swirls of early evening fog in the square of outside garden, forming new misty bits of sculpture around the old mouldering fountain. A drift of breeze sent a branch of the great overhanging pepper tree tapping against the window, and the sound seemed to merge with the music to spell out lovely words at random from her ballet vocabulary. "*Assemble,*" she murmured to the baby, lulled and happy. "*Temp leve . . . sissone . . . port de bras. . . .*"

She caught the baby's sudden, entranced smile in the mirror. Was it possible that somehow he recognized the sounds of these words from his parents', his uncle's, beloved element?

Then turning slowly away from the mirror, she tiptoed down the hall, drawn irresistibly to a closed door. A longing to see some evidence of Rex's taste and temperament as expressed in the place where he lived, where, shut away, he gave himself to the spinning of his dreams, overwhelmed her. Her light touch, before she had even grasped the knob, sent the door slowly, eerily inward. For a second her heart contracted in the thick silence, and her muscles tensed. The baby, sensing danger, cried out. Then she saw it was only the effect of the old, settling house, the listing of walls and floor, that had caused the door to swing open. "It's all right," she soothed the baby as well as herself. "There's no one here."

Cathy stood on the threshold. "We'll just look in," she whispered to Bruce, making the adventure a conspiracy between them.

The windows of the room had once opened to the bay view; now they faced sheer brick wall. There had been an attempt to mask it with a low hanging swag of green-dyed muslin. The walls were also masked with dozens of thumb-tacked ballet programs. Near the door, she could see in the fading light, there was last year's Royal Ballet group, and farther on she recognized, among many pictures, Margot Fonteyn dancing the "Rose Adagio" and doing a *pas de deux* with Michael Somes. Pasted on the mirror was a cutout of printing—a single line. By straining she finally made it out: "The legendary Nijinsky had a record of *entrechat dix*." For a split second her thoughts dwelt on the literal translation, which meant that Nijinsky, a dancer whose levitation has never been equaled, had a record of beating his legs ten times in the air during a single soaring jump. So that was Rex's goal— to rival Nijinsky!

Cathy drew back and closed the door sharply. She had looked too deep, too far. Surely in that one sentence there lay his secret heart, his great ambition, something he thought safe. And she had yielded to curiosity in a way that made her ashamed. For just such curiosity she had scolded Bettina and the younger children at home.

"I guess I'm not a very good person," she whispered to Bruce. Holding the baby's cheek to hers for comfort, she paused in the dark little hallway and leaned against the wall, feeling the cold metal of the old-fashioned wall telephone against her neck. She let her head droop against it because her neck was suddenly tired and her head heavy and aching. "It just sort of shows. I'm trying to be grown up and I'm not at all."

Fidgeting, the baby blew a bubble against her cheek, made her thoughts push out from herself. "Here I am almost crying like a baby myself when I've got you to look after," she said in attempted briskness. But an astonishingly revealing thought held her motionless. Could it be that everyone, no matter how grown up they seemed, sometimes cried out for safety, for comfort, for someone to tell them what to do? She thought of all the frustrations and problems that had been exposed to her in the grown-up world of her family circle, the longing by almost every single one of them for help. There was Rick reaching out, thinking that everything would be solved when Uncle Pat got back. And Cora, Faith, even Walt—all were looking toward the promise of what Uncle Pat's presence and his worldly advice might mean to them. His very name seemed invested with a kind of promise of better things to come for all.

Cathy, too, had counted on Uncle Pat to help her. At least she had been counting on his influence with Dad to see that she got the right ballet teacher. The inescapable truth of her own dependence quickened her breath so that its gasps riffled the soft curling baby hair on Bruce's little head.

The shrilling of the phone so near her released her from thrall. Bruce's tiny mouth stretched into the oval that would mean a scream of fright when he got his breath and could get it out. Cathy picked up the receiver. It could be Rachel at the airport. "Hello."

"Hello! Hello!" There was a pause while a girlish voice—not Rachel's—seemed to gather courage. "Is Rex there?"

Cathy felt herself grinning into the phone. She juggled the baby to ensure his position at her shoulder. Amusement mingled with superiority at being on the receiving end of this call for Rex, but sympathy welled up, too. She said, "Rex is out of town. Do you want to leave a message?"

"Well—" Weighty consideration was obviously tinged with disappointment. "Just say Miriam phoned. Or, never mind, I'll call again. Thanks."

How many girls, Cathy wondered, went through the pleasant agony of phoning Rex every day? Her attention turned back to the baby, her hand automatically registering the fact that he needed changing. "Next to Faith's getting that Paris hat, you're going to be the biggest surprise that's hit her house in years," she confided, giving his tiny flanneled end a gentle pat. Then she went about capably gathering and packing and setting the kitchen to rights before she left. She tried to herd her thoughts into a coherent story to explain Bruce, a story that the family—especially Grandma and Dad, should he return sooner than expected from the medical convention in Chicago—would understand. But she feared that even Gerry's ever-bubbling warmth of enthusiasm might not stretch over the gap of her impulsiveness. The only point of sure acceptance was Cora.

"It'll be easy as pie taking you home to Cora," she

informed Bruce, casting a watchful eye on him propped in his carriage. "Only she won't be satisfied till she's fattened you up." Then reverting her thoughts to the surprise of the Paris hat and the message it had brought to Faith, she said aloud to the baby, "In a way, you know, you're a message to me from Rex." Certainly this would mean the absolute cementing of friendship with Rachel, and the nicest part of it was that she hadn't even been thinking of Rex when she offered to take care of Bruce.

12

Twin Trouble

JOLTING ALONG in a taxi, Cathy looked at the meter and mentally subtracted the sum in her purse from the figure registered there, which grew larger with every passing block. When they drew up in front of Faith's house, Cathy found that she was short a dollar and a half. Of course Faith would give it to her, but she didn't want to dash headlong into the house with Bruce. Cora was the answer.

"Just a minute," she said to the driver. "I have to get some more money." She was thankful for the dark as she hurried along. The baby in her arms was getting restless, for it was well past his six o'clock feeding time. Thank goodness! the formula was ready; all she had to do was give Cora a bottle to heat.

In spite of her need for haste, Cathy paused, startled by a strange rustling in the rhododendrons at the very spot where there had been footprints. Conflicting im-

141

pulses urged her to run and at the same time held her rooted to the walk. All Bettina's imaginative speculation about a diamond thief surged through her thoughts. Protecting the baby from the wind with her body, she leaned forward cautiously. "Who's there?"

The rustling increased, then ceased entirely, followed by a low whuffle of recognition.

"Jimbo! You scoundrel!" As her eyes grew accustomed to the dark, she made out the white circles of his eyes in the mass of dark fur that was almost indistinguishable in the dark shrubbery. What was he doing there? Could he have dug up something? Well, she'd have to come back later and investigate. Hurrying on again, her qualms about bringing Bruce home melted as each footstep brought her closer to the welcoming warmth of the big kitchen and the motherly understanding of Cora's starched, white-aproned vastness.

But the kitchen windows were dark. When she opened the back door to utter stillness and turned on the light, the first thing her gaze registered was a note on the kitchen table saying, "Chicken for dinner is in casserole in oven. Heat half an hour at 350 degrees." On one of the kitchen counters was another note dealing with salad instructions, and scrubbed carrots were in a bowl of water. A fresh cake with a knobby coconut surface gleamed under the transparent cake cover. Even as Cathy's bewildered mind accepted this evidence that Cora would be away that evening, a further note having to do with breakfast instructions, taped on the refrigerator, proclaimed the fact that Cora would not be home in the morning either.

A drawn-out squeal that could only come from Bettina in the throes of either shocked astonishment or merriment came through the house. Then there was the low murmur

that was Faith's responding voice. Cathy stood inde-
cisively staring in dismay at the notes, and wondering
what to do, now that Cora was not there to help.
Automatically she rocked the baby. Then she thought of
the waiting taxi out front. She went hastily up the back
stairs, down the hall to her room, and put the baby on
her bed, swiftly stacking pillows around him so that he
couldn't roll to the edge. With a fervent prayer that he
wouldn't announce his presence with a howl before she
could break the news in her own way, she closed the
door on him and skimmed down the front stairs.

Faith was at the big leather-topped desk in the living
room, her hand on the extension phone as though she
had just hung up. The charged atmosphere said plainly
that she'd been right not to burst in with Bruce in her
arms, for a crisis of some sort was all too apparent.

"Guess what!" Bettina exploded. "It's happened!
Trouble with the twins at camp. She just called and the
nurse in charge of the infirmary says she's never—never
in all her twenty years—seen anything like it."

Cathy's mind picked out the key words of alarm from
all this outpouring. "Nurse? Infirmary? The twins—
Danny and Fran—are they sick?"

"It's been trouble, trouble, trouble with twins all over
the place ever since you left today." As usual, black bangs
flipped as the words popped out; yet the exact situation
was obscured to Cathy with maddening deliberation.
"First Cora's niece Bessie called to say her two sets of
twins have chicken pox, and four kids at once is quite a
chicken poxy house."

Faith added, "So Cora went—"

"But our twins," Cathy broke in, "don't tell me they
have chicken pox?"

"It's Danny," Faith said. "I guess Fran's all right. It's

not chicken pox. Oh, I've never talked to anyone in such a state."

"I could hear her sounding off clear across the room," Bettina added.

"But will you please tell me what this is all about?" Cathy pleaded.

"Well, this dragon, Miss Pinkerton," Bettina went on, "says Danny and Fran raided the camp kitchen last night and found a case of salted peanuts, and they must have taken a coupla pounds with them, and they went out in the woods and Danny sat in some poison ivy while they ate peanuts. And today when they put him in the sick room, he got so mad because the other kids were going on a weenie roast that he bit the foot of an iron bed and deliberately chipped his front tooth. And that isn't all! He's—" She broke off wonderingly as a baby squall floated down from upstairs. "What's that?"

"It's—nothing," Cathy breathed nervously, as uneasy silence met her straining ears. "Go on! What else about Danny?"

"Just that you've got to go up to camp right away," Bettina informed her. "They called and called home, but Mee Chow must still be away on vacation. And then Tess told them to call here. Of course, we told them you'll come, and if you don't they're going to wire Dad in Chicago."

"Oh, no, they mustn't do that," Cathy exclaimed.

"Danny got away from them while everyone was out on the weenie roast," Bettina continued, "and he hid back of the pen where they keep Rosy, the pet pig who eats all the camp garbage. And Miss Pinkerton says if his poison ivy's infected she won't be responsible. But the thing that really threw Miss Pinkerton was hitting her on the back of the neck with a leftover peanut he claimed was a poison dart from a South American blow gun. So you see you've just got to go up right away and get him corraled."

"I didn't think you'd want them to wire your father," Faith said.

"I certainly don't. Not when he's having his first vacation in I don't know how many years, if you call going to a medical convention a vacation." But what was she going to do with Bruce? Gerry was in her office all day; Grandma was too old; Mee Chow was away on vacation. Cathy's wildly circling thoughts brought her back to Faith. A dozen despairing little doubts began to spear their way through her racing thoughts. But further thinking was cut short by the simultaneous ringing of the doorbell, the shrill barking of Jimbo outside, and the piercingly insistent cry of a hungry infant.

"Hey!" Bewilderment and accusation mingled in Bettina's exclamation, and as Cathy darted upstairs in the deafening tempest, she caught a measure of the same expression in Faith's face.

She gathered Bruce in her arms and went back into the hall, where she stopped, tense and uncertain. Looking down toward the first floor as though in a nightmare, she saw the taxi driver deposit the four bulging shopping bags on the mahogany settee in the downstairs hall. "Guess the young lady forgot me," he said. "And that dog—"

Faith collared Jimbo. "He won't bite."

Then there was Bettina's yelp as she investigated the bags. "Diapers! And where did you get that baby?" she demanded, as Cathy appeared.

"It's Rex's nephew," she told them briefly. "I guess I'll have to ask you to pay my taxi fare, Faith."

Faith went to get her purse. Bettina grabbed Jimbo, who still regarded the taxi driver as good material for mincemeat. At the same time, over the din of the baby's shrill cries, Bettina managed to besiege Cathy with questions.

"Hush, now, we'll soon have your bottle," Cathy crooned while one hand fumbled through the bags for the bottled formula. Somehow out of the bedlam the taxi driver was paid, the door closed behind him, and Jimbo settled down with the satisfied sigh of a dog whose work in protecting his family has been well done. The bottle was located and put to warm in the top of the double boiler, and Faith and Bettina sat at the kitchen table waiting for answers to their questions.

Bettina's expression was pained, but Faith's mingled apprehension with something Cathy couldn't quite fathom through the incoherence of her own muddled thoughts. Out of it all, however, one thing was starkly clear: she had to get a bus to camp right away that night. Already she was stepping back into her role as manager of the children. When Danny's temper started winding up, there was no telling what trouble he'd manufacture if he weren't calmed down by someone who understood him.

"There's nothing to it," she concluded, forcing all the assurance she could muster into her tone, when Bruce was finally quietly taking his bottle and she had explained step by step how she had come home with him. Faith and Bettina could certainly take care of Bruce, she reasoned with herself. She turned to Faith. "All you have to do is feed and bathe the baby and see that he gets his naps. There's that old bassinet up in Grandma's attic you can borrow. I'll write out directions."

Bettina's glance roved expressively over Cora's notes. "What do you think we've got already? We'll be lucky if we don't get mixed up and stick the baby in the oven half an hour before dinner and put cod liver oil in the casserole." She turned to Faith. "Maybe it won't be *too* bad. All we really have to do is make his formula, change him every twenty minutes, do his washing. One whole bag of his dipes needs washing right now."

"What could be easier with Faith's automatic washer and dryer down in the basement?" Cathy pointed out.

"But I've never run them. I'm not even sure I've been down in the basement since the machines were installed. And don't you have to sterilize a lot of things?" Faith's helpless, beseeching look above the white cloud of her filmy dress raised Cathy's doubts again.

"If only Cora was here." Bettina swiped at her forehead with the back of her hand. "You *would* have to pick the very most chicken-poxy day of the year to bring home a strange baby."

"But I didn't pick the day," Cathy was thinking. "It was a television producer in Hollywood who really picked the day." And the thought of Rex brought close the memory of Rachel's promise, the sincerity of her tone— "You will dance with Rex, and you will dance very nicely." Cathy came to with a start to hear Bettina say, "I guess we only have to press a button on those machines in the laundry, so our problem is to find out which button and when we do the pressing."

Cathy stood up with determination. "Well, we'll investigate right now." Carefully she laid the baby in Faith's surprised arms. "You hold him like this—and keep this hand on the bottle." Remembering the baby's belligerent resistance when Rachel tried to feed him, Cathy held her breath. Would he take his bottle from Faith? If only she would relax! Stepping back, Cathy gave an involuntary gasp of pleasure as her eyes took in the utter loveliness of Faith's pale gold head close to the baby's tiny, pert, dark one, the curve of her arm, in its transparent sleeve, around the child. How beautiful she was!

"Oh, you look like a magazine cover, Faith," Bettina whispered, overcome with the same awe.

Cathy knew a surge of relief as Bruce went on with his feeding and Faith's body began to lose its tension. Cathy and Bettina found themselves tiptoeing to the basement door for fear of breaking the spell.

Down in the laundry room Bettina spoke of another spell. "You know what I was thinking as we looked at Faith? I was thinking how she's sort of like a fairy princess. You know—the sleeping beauty. I mean, she just isn't hep to what's going on around her. It's as if she lives behind a velvet curtain."

Cathy dumped the shopping bag of baby clothes in the washing machine. Her thoughts traveled back to the word Gerry had used about Faith: "Ineffectual." The sleeping beauty was a nicer label. If only Uncle Pat would come home soon! "What was it that happened to the sleeping beauty?" she mused aloud.

"You know," Bettina reminded. "The handsome prince kissed her and woke her from her enchanted sleep."

The word "ineffectual" stayed with Cathy, carrying its troubling train of worry to the further difficulties she encountered at the bus terminal. The bus she should have been on had just left; another was not due to leave for three hours. That one would bring her into camp at midnight, and in the meantime Miss Pinkerton might become discouraged and phone Dad in Chicago.

She turned back to the seat where she had left her overnight bag and the box that held Cora's big fresh coconut cake that Faith had sent along for the children.

She could phone Walt, but she didn't want to, since she wasn't ready yet to disclose her impulsiveness in taking Bruce to Faith's. Maybe Gerry would drive her over. But the ringing phone in Gerry's office brought no answer. A call to Gerry's apartment seemed about to have the same disappointing result, then on the twelfth ring there was Gerry's breathless voice.

"Cathy—wait till I start to breathe again. I heard the phone coming up in the elevator and thought I wouldn't get here in time. . . . Of course I'll pick you up and drive you over," she said, when she had heard the account of trouble with Danny at camp. "You be out there on the curb, and I'll be along in ten minutes."

It was ten minutes to the dot when Cathy stepped gratefully into the yellow convertible. The smell of its newness rose pleasantly around her, as its quiet power in Gerry's capable hands sped them off into the night.

"Much as I'd like to, I can't stay at camp with you," Gerry told her. "I've got a date—a late one, fortunately— and as soon as I deliver you I'll have to turn right around and hurry home to dress. But you'll know better what to do about Danny than I would, anyway." Gerry tossed her a warming sidewise glance. "Children just instinctively know you have a way with them."

It was the second time that day Cathy had heard almost these identical words. Now the scene when Rachel had spoken them came back, and she remembered the meeting of their eyes, Rachel's trust in leaving Bruce with her and her own promise to take good care of him. But in a short time she was leaving him in the hands of a twelve-year-old and a person who might be classed as "grown-up" but actually wasn't as capable of dealing with emergencies as the twelve-year-old. Yet Cathy's allegiance to her own family, to the brothers and sisters she had watched over for so long, had greater urgency.

All at once she found herself thinking aloud and relating to Gerry the afternoon episode with Rachel and Bruce, her feeling of betraying a trust by leaving Bruce behind. "Yet I had to leave him, and it's strange, but I'm almost glad to go. I guess I hadn't realized how—well—how homesick I've been for the children."

"I know," Gerry said sympathetically. "Your roots have been pretty firmly fixed with those five youngsters."

That was one of the most satisfying things about Gerry. You could open up an interior conversation and have her follow right along as though she'd been with you all the time. "I hadn't realized how terribly I've missed them—even the twins' tantrums," she wound up, leavening her concern with an attempt at humor. As she spoke, her mind rushed ahead impatiently to the rebel that was Danny, to Fran, to Tess, and to Pipper; at the same time part of her stretched back to the baby boy at Faith's.

"If you'll pardon the expression," Gerry observed, "you're like a faithful, adoring dog being whistled two ways."

Cathy smiled in spite of her anxiety. "Exactly," she agreed.

The car had to idle in bridge traffic. Gerry took this opportunity to pull up the hood of her yellow cashmere coat. "I love having the top of the car down, but this wind's a bit on the sharp side. Here," she urged, taking a silk square from the glove compartment, "better tie this around your head. You don't want to complicate things any further by catching cold."

As Cathy obeyed, she looked out to where the Alcatraz Island beacon flashed its moving silver circle on the roll-

ing slither of dark bay, lighting the bulk of vast black
tankers and the sleek majesty of moored battleships.
Ahead were the shimmering lights of Oakland; behind
was the brilliant night glitter of her own city. And suspended there, momentarily motionless on the great steel
structure between the two, eyes following her heart's
longing, she looked back to the beckoning spotlight that
revealed the whiteness of Coit Tower, placing Telegraph
Hill for her on the shore line.

She said, "Right there on the south slope of Telegraph
Hill is where Rex lives. Now in a few days when Rex
and Rachel get back, I'll be there again, and this time
I'll really dance with Rex. I really will! Rachel promised."
The rising tide of happiness was so strong within her that
the words tumbled out breathlessly.

"The whole hill seems to have a kind of halo of glory
and suspense for you, doesn't it?"

"Yes, it does," Cathy breathed.

There was significant understanding for Cathy in the
little pause that followed, and then Gerry said, "Well, I
certainly look forward to meeting Rex. You'll have to
bring him up to my apartment some evening."

"Rachel, too," Cathy urged. "She's like no one I've ever
known, Gerry. So friendly and sweet, and so wonderfully
talented—Why, that sounds like a description of you—"
she broke off in surprise. "Only, she's different, somehow.
Which sounds mixed up. I guess I am mixed up," she
concluded. "Will I ever get over this feeling of being
whistled two ways, as you put it? Will I ever be *me*
again, settled and sure, calmly belonging in just one
place?"

"Maybe you haven't found the real *you* yet," Gerry
observed. "That's something I don't know. But think

how awful—how bleak—if nothing whistled to you at all, if you lived in a static state like Faith."

Well, one thing was certain, there was nothing static about Gerry. She drank in all of life with gusty delight. For her there was no sipping, no tentative tasting as there was for Faith. Even Gerry's most serious moods seemed to hold a background of laughter and light-heartedness.

Then abruptly the car was in gear and speeding ahead again as the traffic got under way. Cathy felt the lulling movement of the motor's purr. She forced her hands to take a firmer grip on the cake box in her lap; worn out from the strain of the day, her head drooped against the collar of her corduroy coat. "I'll just stay overnight at camp, spend the morning with Danny, and get back to Faith's tomorrow afternoon," she murmured. "Nothing can happen to Bruce overnight. Nothing at all. . . ."

"Of course it can't," Gerry reassured.

Then just as she felt herself slipping into sleep she thought she heard someone say, "Hello, Lefty." Why, that's Walt! She made an heroic effort to turn her head. "Imagination," she mumbled drowsily. She knew that he wasn't there; yet somehow she felt that he was—or he would have been if she had let him. "If you don't mind, I'll just rest here a minute," she was dreamily trying to tell him, as she seemed to feel the solid pillow of his broad shoulder under her head. "And then I'll help you shell prune pits."

Vaguely she was aware of the car's slackening speed and of Gerry's hand reaching out from the wheel to pull up the scarf that the wind had blown back from her head. The reality of Gerry and the dream figure of Walt confusedly melted together. She tried to keep awake just long enough to say something else, but it kept sliding away from her through the weaving, dark mistiness of sleep. And then at last she knew—it was Jimbo and the rhododendron bush. She'd meant to look there again before she left.

13

Quandary at Camp

CATHY DIDN'T KNOW that it would be three days before she could think of leaving camp. On that first night she learned that Danny's poison ivy hadn't been infected by his visit to Rosy's pen, but it had spread. Although he wasn't really sick, he was fretful and fussy with the bottled-up energy of any ten-year-old whose every ruffian impulse was stimulated by the thwarted desire to scratch, by boredom, and by the natural longing of a half-sick child for the familiarity of home.

"He's downright cantankerous," Miss Pinkerton, the camp nurse, explained, as they walked to a cabin set off by itself. "As a matter of fact, I've never worked so hard before to keep a child out of mischief." Miss Pinkerton's **voice** sounded brusquely angry and frustrated and a little **ash**amed.

It must be humiliating to have to admit to a small boy's older sister that she'd let herself get hopelessly frazzled, Cathy decided sympathetically.

"Danny's the only one in the infirmary now. That's part of his trouble," Miss Pinkerton admitted with a sigh of exasperation. "He's missed company."

"Could I sleep there with him?" Cathy asked and had her answer at once in the relief that seemed to ooze from every pore of Miss Pinkerton's thin, harried face. Miss Pinkerton stopped abruptly under a light hanging from a tree, surprise in her glance. "I thought you'd be older. That is, I got that impression from the children talking about you."

Cathy felt herself flush under the close scrutiny of the older woman. "I can imagine. This is the first time they've ever been away from me. But I have a feeling that it's been good for them." She paused, part of her thoughts darting off as usual to the strange idea that somehow they were going to have to do without her a great deal from now on.

They walked on. That rosy glow touching the sky beyond a group of cabins was certainly a camp fire. The distant sounds that her ears were sorting out gradually separated into the counselor's whistle, the buzz and squeal of children finishing their evening sing. As they entered the cabin of their destination, Cathy was the center of such close-up tumultuous squeals, the target of such a catapulting onslaught of small arms and legs and eager young faces buried against her that she felt as though she had been tackled by an entire football team. She barely managed to save the cake by holding it aloft. "Where did you all come from? How did you know—?"

"Ever since we knew you were coming we've taken turns watching at the front gate," Fran explained.

Cathy was gasping for breath after another round of hugs, including the redly poison-ivied Danny. And then, the board with its picture puzzle moved aside, she settled on the edge of the bed, little Pipper on her lap, his arms tight around her neck. She heard Miss Pinkerton say briskly, "All right now, you have half an hour with your sister." Then to Cathy, "They have to be in their own quarters at nine, lights out at nine-thirty. I'll be back to see about your bed here."

"Golly!" Danny exploded happily. "You're going to sleep with me here?"

"Tomorrow night you'll have to sleep in our cabin," Tess and Fran insisted.

"How about my cabin?" Pipper demanded. "Know what, Cathy? They've got me in a baby cabin. It isn't fair. I'm almost six."

Cathy held him off for inspection. A choking wave of love made her voice waver. "You've grown, too. Why, you're huge. Must be the Mount Diablo air and the food."

Danny held his nose. "Don't mention the food here. What I'd give for some of Mee Chow's apple dumplings!"

"I'd even eat Mee Chow's oatmeal without a squawk," Fran tacked on expressively.

Cathy's hand went out to touch Tess, their quiet one. Their nine-year-old bookworm, as the other children called her.

"Tess is going to get the prize for her nature study notebook," Pipper announced proudly. "She knows more flowers and birds and butterflies than anybody."

"She won't get *all* the prizes," Fran deprecated. "I'm getting better and better every day at diving; and I'm making a tie rack for Dad."

"I'm weaving a potholder for Mee Chow," Pipper told her. "It's wed."

Cathy smiled to hear his *r*'s still sounding like *w*'s. It was a shock to realize they had been separated only a little more than a week.

Danny's pajamaed shoulders swaggered in a sheepish attempt at bravado. "I guess I'll win some kind of an old prize for being bad."

"Danny's been the worst—the very worst—boy they've ever had here. Of course, Miss Pinkerton doesn't know that chip out of his tooth has really been out for a long time." Fran's relish in proclaiming this news was cut short by a reproving glance from Cathy.

"Squealer! Telling on your own twin—"

Cathy cut the taunt short by bringing out the cake. Danny's pocket knife was put into action, and the paper napkins used in packing the cake served as plates. But there was something else that had to be told.

"You tell our plan, Tess. Go ahead." Breaths were held, and eagerness and suppressed excitement danced in every face. Cathy was amused, as their old strategy was put into action. Whenever they wanted something really important, really special, they got Tess to do the asking, Tess, who almost never asked for anything for herself, and who was so withdrawn, so gently content to live in her beloved world of birds and flowers that she was sometimes forgotten in the boisterous clamor of the others.

The delicacy, the gravity, the reserve of the small face, beneath the silky fair hair with its center part, touched Cathy with new awareness. "Why, she's a small edition of Faith! That mustn't be!" she thought. She'd have to see that Tess joined in more games. She'd spend more time with her, draw her out; and at the same time she'd have to guard against the twins' jealousy. Attention had to be equally allotted where they were concerned. She knew their little quirks—the exasperations, the frustrations, the eagerness for attention and affection which sparked a flare of "badness." This year she'd buckle down with Dad and Mee Chow to a program of help for the twins, too. She stopped aghast. How could she do all this when she needed time for herself—for her career?

As though divining the struggle in her sister, Tess asked finally, "What's the matter?"

Cathy swallowed. "Nothing."

"Of course, there's nothing the matter, silly," Fran spoke around a mouthful of cake. "Go ahead. Ask her."

Thus prodded, Tess began tentatively, "Well, we've been learning how to camp."

"Every week one cabin goes on an overnight trip with sleeping bags and everything," Danny burst out, unable to contain himself.

Fran added, "We cook on a real camp fire."

"We are very careful with matches," Pipper announced solemnly. And then because Tess still shyly hesitated to disclose what all this was leading to, as though he couldn't stand the popping strain of the secret one more moment, he drew a deep breath and let it out. "So next week when you have your birthday and get the car Dad promised, we're all going camping together. A camping trip just for us!"

"Oh," Cathy said awkwardly, "well—" The radiance on the circle of faces was too much to bear. She had to look away, down at the floor, marking time by easing her feet out of their low-heeled sling pumps. Where were the words to tell them that she wasn't going to have a car, that she was going to ask for ballet lessons instead? Staring at her stockinged feet, she seemed to see them in her pink ballet slippers, and then, curiously, she saw the row of hard-worn ballet shoes against a wall in Rex's room. For a brief instant the aura of that room with its mementoes of ballet was overwhelming, blotting out all else.

Then even more curiously she felt herself slipping back

to early childhood, wondering if she had ever wanted anything as much as these children wanted her to have a car to take them camping. From a remote corner of that past, memory brought the picture of a particular picnic. Pipper hadn't even been born. Her mother had carried Tess, the baby, Dad had carried a play pen for the twins, and she had been assigned to watch Bettina. There had been a pink carnation at the throat of her mother's blouse—she could almost breathe its sun-warmed spice again, almost see the pleasure in her mother's face as she took it off and handed it to Tess to play with. "How this baby loves flowers," her mother would always say.

Lifting her head now, looking at Tess, who knew more flowers than anybody, as Pipper pointed out, she saw the child's small hand offering something she'd been guarding carefully, hands behind her back.

"Oh, another corsage," Fran hooted, reaching to bat at a mosquito. "Honestly, Cathy, she just makes these all day long, and it's only some old weedy daisies with their stems in tin foil off a candy bar."

"It's pretty," Pipper praised sportingly.

"It's lovely," Cathy said, taking the tiny nosegay—a daisy and wild fern center artfully arranged with a border of plushy ageratum, amethyst blue.

Tess's smile was like a flash of sunlight, speaking adoration, a wordless happiness. Then swiftly it faded, as though once more she divined Cathy's troubled state.

"You will take us camping?" Danny demanded, impatient with this diversion.

"I'd like to," Cathy groped in stumbling inadequacy. Outside the evening insects sang their summer night's song that blended with the children's voices in the distance. Inside the moths flung themselves at the light bulbs in crazy loops. "But I'm not really counting on a car. We'll have to see."

"Dad promised you one on your seventeenth birthday. He wouldn't go back on a promise." Pipper's voice scaled upward to the verge of passionate tears.

Cathy rocked him soothingly. "No. No, of course not." Her conscience smote her at the false impression of her tone. Now was the time to be honest, to tell them why she wouldn't have a birthday present of a car, but somehow she couldn't quite do it.

Tess pressed against Cathy's knee, large-eyed, constrained as though she braced herself, braced all of them for disappointment. "Maybe you don't want a car. Maybe there's a reason?" Her last supposition was a barely audible whisper, tense, despairing, but oddly accepting even before the explanation was given. "She's the only one who'll really understand," Cathy thought. "She's the only one who'll look through her own world into mine."

Behind them the door creaked. Miss Pinkerton, good humor restored by Cathy's presence, said brightly, "Bedtime, children. Bedtime."

"But you haven't promised about our camping trip," Fran insisted. "Promise before we go. Promise. Please promise!"

Cathy got up, making her voice as light, as easy as possible over the oppression that weighed heavily on her. "We'll see tomorrow." Tomorrow she'd have to find the courage to tell them.

14

Black is the Color
of My True Love's Hair

THE NEXT TWO DAYS were happily, exhaustingly kaleidoscopic. "It's the soft life I've been living at Faith's," she would tell the children when she began to sag by mid-afternoon. Actually she'd forgotten how astonishing the demands of her brood could be. Each one clamored for her to be in on his or her particular activity at the same time. Since camp life was devised to keep each child busy at his own level at all hours, Cathy was torn between nature hikes, basketball, swimming and diving lessons, handcraft of three separate and intriguing kinds, and, in addition to everything else, the real purpose of her stay, her trips to the infirmary where Danny was subdued, if not exactly blissful, as long as she was there to play or read to him or just to change the compresses on his legs.

Now and then in all this besieging busy-ness she had found time to think about Bettina and Faith and Bruce. Once she had phoned, but the hubbub of children around the camp phone had prevented her hearing anything more from Bettina than the brief assurance that all was well.

But through everything there were the dark bits of worry that had to do with not finding the right moment to tell the children about the car and that their plans of a camping trip would have to be given up. She knew that sheer longing had made them take her silence for the affirmative answer they wanted. She kept finding escape for her conscience by telling herself that she'd settle things with Dad first, that she'd see what he said about the car versus ballet training. Then on the third day Danny's poison ivy was definitely better, and Miss Pinkerton said he might join the other children for play. Cathy was free to go home.

She stepped back into San Francisco's cool bright windiness feeling outwardly browned and hardened by the strenuous three days of summer camp and disturbingly unsettled and crumbling at the edges inside. The transplantation into such an all-consuming swirl of activity had kept this life at Faith's, with its problems and mysteries, from seeming real. Now, separated from camp life by the intervening miles, she felt once more the keen responsibility for Rachel's baby, the pressure of her promise there, with all of its undercurrent of closeness to Rex, to the world of ballet, and to the rapturous pull of her own career.

For a last moment before she entered the house she paused, holding tight to the doorknob, and tried to sort through the jumble of thought and feeling that stirred her. Abruptly her attention was diverted to the corner of the house. A windblown motion of the shrubbery, showering the sweet rich fragrance of its blossoms on the air, suddenly recalled the incident of Jimbo's growl there in the dark the night she had brought Rachel's baby home.

There was no sound of the dog now. But there was something else. She moved from the porch, ears straining, and caught an unidentifiable thudding sound, repeated again and again, perhaps a dozen times and then stopping. It came, as nearly as she could tell, from the foundation of the house. Her hand trembled a little and she felt a shivery tremor of adventure as she parted the bushes. She was getting as dramatically imaginative as Betts, she thought, and Bettina's theory of a diamond thief huddled in this exact spot returned to her.

She and Bettina had searched so carefully for clues that there wasn't a chance they'd missed anything. But what could Jimbo have wanted here? And what was the riddle of the thudding noise? "Oh, my glory!" she said aloud. So that's it! Jimbo's chewing shoe—his present from the meter reader. She remembered how he had brought it to them proudly. So that was what Jimbo was growling over, worrying, the other night. But it didn't explain the muffled, rhythmic sounds she'd just heard. Sounds that were repeated now, their tempo steady, as she stood there. Then all was still save for the crisp call of a mockingbird in a nearby cypress. She looked up to see the flip of its wedge-shaped tail and the neat white underside.

Listening again intently, she heard the rhythmic thumping sounds repeated, and at the same time she heard something else—a sound as startling as it was sweet. The long-stilled sound of Faith's harp in the rill of a soft arpeggio, followed by the further surprise of Faith's voice in song.

Cathy went in and closed the front door softly behind her. The bassinet from Grandma's attic stood in front of a drowsy fire; a small arm waved above its edge. Faith at her harp patterned the room with the gold and whiteness that seemed a part of her fragile beauty. Her hair was loosely done in a new fashion, its silky sweep falling forward and glinting gold against the metallic brightness of the harp. The gold and white were repeated in the quaint flower print of her full-skirted dress.

Cathy stood quietly, listening as Faith sang an old folk song:

> Black is the color of my true love's hair,
> His face is something wondrous fair;
> And still I hope the day will come
> When he and I will be as one.

The poignancy of the words and the spirit in which they were sung caught at Cathy. With a sudden understanding of Grandma's rage at Uncle Pat, she found herself praying a beseeching little prayer: "Please let Uncle Pat and Faith be happy together again. Please!"

Jimbo was the first to be aware of Cathy's presence. Stretched beside the bassinet, he blinked benignly at Cathy and then laboriously got up and came to her. Cathy reached down to give him a pat.

"Cathy!" Faith came to greet her. "How are you? How are the children at camp? Danny?"

"They're fine, all fine." The baby made a little sound; Cathy took an involuntary step toward him; she checked herself as Faith picked him up and smoothed his back, his dark, elfin head nestled against her neck.

"He was a little out of sorts the day you left, and that

night I was petrified when he woke three times. But now he's just an angel. Hear him," she commanded softly. "He's cooing."

Cathy not only heard the happy baby with pleasure and relief, but she heard Faith with utter amazement. It was as though she had peeled off layers of reserve and had come alive with a quiet glow.

"I had no idea babies could be such fun, such little individuals." There was a reflective pause, and then Faith said with a trace of her old shyness, "Cathy, my dear, I must thank you for leaving this little fellow with me. I think he's done me good."

"I think he has, too," Cathy exulted. "And it's so wonderful to hear your harp again, and you singing. It sounded just lovely."

"I hadn't realized how I missed playing," Faith acknowledged. Then her glance followed Cathy's to the blue marshmallow box on the piano. "I found that back in the music cabinet. Gerry told me to find it and look inside. Pat and I toasted marshmallows that last night, and there was a funny little poem he wrote then that I didn't understand. It was meant to be humorous, I guess, but I took it all too personally, too seriously, and was hurt. I didn't know that Pat wrote a last stanza after I went to bed." A deep flush rose to her cheeks. "He put it in with the marshmallows, and then he put the box away in the music cabinet, thinking I'd find it when I got out my music, I suppose." Her voice hesitated. "Only, I lost my interest in my music and didn't want to play for so long. If only I'd found this long ago—"

Faith's shoulders straightened, her new mood conveyed by the briskness of her hands as they folded a blanket, by the alive tenderness in her glance as she looked at the baby, and in the intuitive way he yielded full trust to a moment of cuddling before she put him back in the bassinet.

Cathy could only guess what the poem had said to Faith. There was so much Cathy wanted to say about Uncle Pat, but she didn't quite know how. Instead she just asked, "Is Cora back?"

Faith said, "Not yet. But do you know Bettina's turned out to be a really wonderful cook? She's down in the basement now doing the baby laundry. That's taken hours. I had no idea. . . . She's been a dear about sticking to it. I guess she'll be glad Bruce has to go home today." She sighed a little sigh of real regret. "Oh, I'll miss him so!"

"You mean Rachel's home? She called?"

Faith nodded. "Bettina hated to tell her you were away. We thought it might worry her, so she doesn't know you had to go to camp. Only if you hadn't gotten home by three, we were going to have to take him over ourselves."

"By three?" A glance at her watch told her that it was only an hour away.

Faith pushed back her hair. "I guess I haven't explained very carefully. The baby's mother and her brother—is that Rex?—got home less than an hour ago, and they called to see if you could bring Bruce back and stay for a dancing lesson this afternoon."

So Rex was home. She'd been saying maybe today, maybe tomorrow, for so long, it seemed, and now it was *now*. Once again that wavelike sound of music filled her ears, lifting her upward, rushing her into the familiar dream of dancing with Rex. "I'll have to get ready," she managed unsteadily, "and I'll run down in the basement and see Betts."

She saw Bettina through a gauzelike veil of emotion.

She saw the small brown arm raised with its racquet to bat a tennis ball against the laundry room wall. Vaguely her mind registered the fact that this batting noise was what she'd heard outside the house.

Bettina turned, racquet suspended. "Hi! How are the kids at camp? How's Danny's poison ivy and his chipped tooth?"

"His poison ivy's all gone, and his tooth just had that same little chip it's had since he fell on his face skating last winter."

"Trust Danny to get that Pinkerton's goat by having her think he did it there." Bettina swiped at her bangs with the back of her hand. "Well, what do you think of Faith?"

"It's a miracle," Cathy said.

"I had it all doped out almost as soon as you left the other day. I just figured if I left her alone with the baby she might snap out of some of her daziness. Grandma had the same idea. We went over there to get the bassinet, and Grandma just about popped her buttons at first when she heard you'd dumped a strange baby on us."

"I expect she made quite a scene," Cathy agreed.

"But then when she saw Faith holding him, and that new look she was starting to get, she called me back and told me to make myself scarce so Faith would have to change his diaper and feed him and stuff, and it certainly worked." Bettina twirled her tennis racquet. "I just concentrated on our food and making Bruce's formula, and of course it was easy to pretend it took ages to do the baby's washing. Gave me a chance to uncramp my forehand down here—sort of uncramp my problem, too."

Cathy turned to a pile of freshly laundered tiny shirts and gowns and began to fold them. They would have to be packed. She ought to get started. The clean scent surged softly around her and merged with her happiness as her hands worked. And then she realized Bettina's last statement hung in the air, inviting a probing question. "Your problem?"

Bettina flopped herself down on the mangle bench, batting the tip of a soiled sneaker with her racquet. "I guess I just began thinking how you were only thirteen when Mama died and you had to take over, and how I'm practically thirteen, and the twins are too old to be scrapping like Indians all the time. I mean they ought to be helping me look after Tess and Pipper so you could have time for practicing your ballet lessons and concentrating on your career without fussing over who gets hurt or mad or into trouble at school." She paused, fanning her chest with her striped T shirt as though the effort of putting this decision into words had sent her into a clammy sweat. "I mean," she finished unequivocally, "Faith isn't the only one around here who needed to get hep to herself. I guess I did, too."

Cathy wanted to put her arms around Bettina and kiss the top of her head the way Gerry would have done so easily, but it would have embarrassed them both. And just then Bettina broke the solemn moment by tacking on cheerfully, "By the way, Walt's called a jillion times. I promised him you'd call the minute you got in. He's got a keen idea he wants to tell you about."

But Cathy hardly heard her. Walt always had an idea to talk over. This time it would have to wait. She took another quick glance at her watch and gathered an armload of folded baby clothes. Time was fleeting; she had to rush.

15

New Sights

SINCE FAITH SAID she would drive Cathy over but could not wait while she had her lesson, Bettina decided to go along. So all three, with Bruce in Cathy's arms, the bags of baby paraphernalia in back, rounded the curve on Telegraph Hill just at three. There it seemed as though the same pair of spotted sandpipers strutted on the old fountain's central cherub. The windward list of the house, its weathered board siding darkly shadowed among the great new apartment houses, seemed even crazier seen through Faith's and Bettina's eyes.

But there was comfort, too, in Faith's and Bettina's presence in the hurdle of the first moment of meeting, for no sooner had the car stopped than Rachel and Rex came out to claim Bruce, to unload the packages, to welcome Cathy.

Her mouth had gone cottony at the sight of both Rex and Rachel running down the steps and through the old

169

garden to meet them and she couldn't say a word. But
no one noticed that she didn't speak. Bettina's enthusiastic
introductions, Faith's smile, her gracious greeting, her
affectionately murmured good-bys to Bruce filled in every
pause.

"Oh, he looks wonderful—almost a little plump—"
Rachel cooed in the excited pleasure of having her baby
back. The scarlet hibiscus tucked in her dark hair and
the satiny sheen of her slender dark arms glinted in the
sun as she reached into the car and claimed Bruce. Her
dark eyes spilled over with warm friendship and with
happy gratitude.

Then there was Rex's face just above hers as they
walked back through the garden, his arms laden with
shopping bags. "It was so good of you to keep the baby,
and he looks wonderful. Things worked out just right
after Rachel came south. I hope you'll see our film some
day on TV. We're so glad you could come this afternoon
for a lesson."

One after the other the sentences rolled out into the
gusty summer air, each one seemingly fraught with
special meaning and originality for Cathy. Rex's charm,
his lithe dancer's grace, the odd, slanting beauty of his
eyes were just as Cathy had pictured them a thousand
times. In their few steps together so close, she felt again
the strange mixture of hero worship and tremulous awe
and her own repeated honest wonderment at how Rex
could have singled her out from all the other dancers in
the festival at school, at how he could have remembered
her and actually wanted to dance with her.

A frond from the old, overhanging pepper tree trailed
across her cheek, leaving its pungent perfume. For a
moment at the door, while his package-laden arm reached
out, fumbling for the knob, and she bent forward to help,

there was a rapt moment of their hands colliding. Then he stepped back for her to enter, and in another instant he had gone through to the back room with his load, followed by Rachel and the baby.

To Cathy's astonishment there were three other girls waiting, all in practice clothes, one limbering up at the *barre,* the two others sitting on the red couch talking. Even in the brief space it took Rex to walk past them Cathy was aware of a change in the girls. It was as though the whole shadowed room, its faint rosy light strained through red casement curtains, had sprung into immediate brilliance; each girl was more vitally alive somehow, yet hushed in his presence. Then as he disappeared the trio relaxed.

"You just starting lessons?" one girl asked Cathy in a friendly way.

Cathy nodded, busied herself at tying on her toe shoes, a bleak heaviness enveloping her. So this was to be a class—four girls together. A class! Well, what had she expected? A lesson is a lesson. Lessons can mean classes.

As though in extension of this line of thought one of the girls at the mirror inquired of her companion, "Did Rex come to your house for your first lesson?"

Regarding the curve of her slim round neck, the lissom line of her legs in the mirror, the other replied, "Of course. I guess he always does. He has to win over the parents. Most folks wouldn't pay a fellow that young for lessons; but when they see him dance—" She raised her arms and took a measured step. She seemed to throw her reflection a fond, if somewhat abstracted, glance of admiration. "I remember how thrilled I was when he told me I had a nice lightness, a natural rhythmic sense, and the ideal figure for a dancer." She finished with a small, amused giggle.

"Part of his sales talk," the other girl agreed. "Not that you haven't got the ideal figure," she acceded in encouragement. "He even told me he'd like me to work with him on an original dance."

The first girl said, "You can't really blame him. A little sales promotion's fair enough in every line. And after all you've got to admire his devotion to Rachel."

Unmoving, head hunched over her ballet shoes, Cathy's mind refused to accept the jetting coldness of the words.

"Ivan Harkoff gives him a free lesson every day because he's such a genius. But he and Rachel have their expenses here, and he's got to make money as well as study. I've heard him say several times that he's going to stick by Rachel until her husband gets back."

Cathy's thoughts doubled back to that so-called sales talk that Rex had used with her, words she had heard there on the school stage. They had been her very own, cherished, looked at from every angle until they had assumed shape and substance. Now they hung in space before her as someone else's also, and their very shape and substance gave them the power to batter her with a jolting shock. The blows didn't really hurt—yet; right now she was too numb. The hurt would come later when she could feel again.

The girl at the *barre* had a short, stubby shock of blondish hair. The measured, padding sound of her slippered feet, agile, assured, seemed to keep time in an absurd way with the faint hunger protests of little Bruce coming from the back of the house.

Equally absurd, Cathy thought, was the way the girl's blond head enlarged and blurred and became Walt's head. "Every guy has a line of some kind he hands out," Walt was saying, like a record being played back. His voice, his very inflection, blended with the beat of the dancer's feet, shattering Cathy's dream into shapelessness, humiliation. All these thoughts had probably occupied no more than ten ticks of Cathy's watch; yet as Rex returned, ready for the lesson, she felt that eons had passed.

The girls, charged with new vitality, lined up at the *barre*, Cathy moving with them. The brilliance that Rex's presence had brought before was obviously still there for the other girls, but it had been misted over for Cathy. Somehow the springiness had gone from her muscles. Her legs and arms seemed to be propelled mechanically through the familiar warming-up exercises by the same push-button force that activated one of Walt's inventions.

One by one the girls stepped out for solo work, and one by one they finished, transfigured, flushed by triumph or manifestly impatient with their shortcomings. At last Cathy took her turn. She saw the unveiled curiosity in the glances of the other girls. As though looking at someone else, she saw her reflection in the long mirror, her arms and legs sun-browned from the days of outdoor living at camp, the dusting of freckles over her nose sun-deepened now, the coppery brown of her hair faintly sun-bleached. The outline of her figure seemed somewhat too slender compared with the other girls'. She saw Rex's eyes on her, aloof, concentrated.

In a second, now, she told herself, she would feel the pull of his force that had helped her to dance with such miraculous ease before. But this time there was no guiding touch. The mysterious power just wasn't forthcoming. For an eternity she stood waiting, and then at his command she stepped out. She faltered, wobbling on point, her arms stiff, her head and eyes turned toward the floor as though they had wills of their own and refused to follow the carriage of her arms as they should. Her *arabesque* was released too quickly with an exasperating jerk and her follow-through was awkward.

"A first lesson is always difficult. Next time you'll be more at ease." Rex's voice was not unkind, not unencouraging. But Cathy's heart did not take its leap of delight. In the basic movement of her *battements retirés* she felt her hip rise when her knee lifted, certainly a glaring error in one of the most elementary exercises. Too late she made the effort to keep both hips straight and even. Rex's correction with what seemed an ill-concealed effort of patience only added to her feeling of hopelessness.

She didn't know how she got through the rest of her lesson. All she knew was that she had to get away, alone, out in the evening fog where she could let the tears come until she was wrung dry of disillusionment and could find herself, her real self, again.

But she couldn't leave quickly after all, because, when she was dressed and had her slippers and practice clothes in their bag, Rachel appeared and asked her into the kitchen.

"I don't feel that I've really thanked you enough for keeping Bruce." The straight grace of her back rested a moment against the sink; and then she moved to the stove to prepare a cup of tea that Cathy was sure she couldn't swallow. "After I was on my way the other day I thought that I must be out of my mind to leave Bruce with someone I'd just met. And then do you know—" her dark eyes looked directly at Cathy again with their message of friendship—"I just thought of the way you had with him, how he seemed to sense instinctively that you understood him. And I thought of everything you had told me about your life at home, looking after your five brothers and sisters, and the real happiness in your face as you talked,

and I felt reassured. Oh, Cathy, I'll never forget what
you've done for me." With a quick motion she urged
Cathy to sit at the small table. Something in the girl's
suddenly tautened muscles intrigued Cathy out of her
self-absorption so that the pinched hurt in her chest was
momentarily lessened.

"We enjoyed having Bruce," Cathy told her. "He's a
sweet baby." She thought about telling Rachel the truth
about leaving him with Faith and Bettina, but before she
could speak, Rachel said, "It's given me an idea. You
see, I've been offered a chance to take over a class of tiny
children, but the very thought of it terrifies me. I haven't
the patience or even any notion of how to keep them
quiet and interested, and I thought you could help me—
be my assistant." Unconsciously she had reached across
the table, her slender hand palm up with an insistent
asking grace of its own.

In her utter bewilderment Cathy could only stumble,
"But didn't you see my lesson just now? Why, I was
terrible."

"I looked in for a moment. You weren't terrible at all.
You were just frightened—nervous—very tense." Rachel
gently smiled. "Rex is an artist, not a teacher, really."
She sighed, her dark eyes abruptly clouding. "We need
pupils; we really need the money." She leaned toward
Cathy again, persuasively. "You see how it is, Cathy?
I mustn't turn down this opportunity. Little children
respond to you. You have a way with them that I know
nothing about. You can help me make my class a real
success. I can't pay you, but I'll give you lessons. Or
Rex will if you prefer. And you're welcome to bring your
little sisters to the class."

"Tess," Cathy breathed in eagerness. "Tess would
love it, and it's just what she needs. And maybe Bettina

and Fran, too. Oh, it would be fun!" The satisfying sensation, the expectancy of having her feet on firm ground now was like a cool breeze blowing over the hurt inside, easing it for the time being. "I'd like to help you," she said. "I'd like to very much."

Rachel said reflectively, "In a way experience of this kind could be a testing ground. You might even decide later on to take up teaching as a career. I don't mean of dancing, necessarily, unless that appeals to you."

The day was darkening. The only light in the room was a pale silver square barred with purple shadows that came through the high, old-fashioned window. There was a stage-set feeling about it that seemed the perfect setting for Rachel's exotic appeal. Cathy was aware of gratitude for Rachel's friendship, for this kind offer. But the enthusiasm that had gone into her acceptance seemed suddenly to drain away. "I'll have to go now, Rachel. Thanks for asking me."

"I'll call you," Rachel said. "We'll want to work out a class routine together before we start on Saturday."

Cathy nodded in withdrawn politeness, edging away. Hesitating at the front door, she filled her eyes with a last spellbound glimpse of Rex rehearsing his own dance, his concentration undisturbed by her presence. The superb confidence, the polished flow of power still moved her to the same flame of awe she had experienced that day on the stage at school. In encouraging her he hadn't meant to be unkind. It was just a matter of expedience, of business necessity. It was she who had sold herself a bill of goods, as Walt had put it.

She guided the door softly behind her, its faint closing click part of the closing of all the reveries, the ecstatic daydreams. Had she really believed that Rex wanted her to be his partner? To dance professionally with him?

"Set your sights high, but face your limitations squarely."
The refrain of Miss Allison's pet slogan for her gym classes
ran through Cathy's mind. And there was the follow-up
to that slogan in her little speech to Cathy that last day
at school: "Remember there's a chance for growth in
hero worship." Well, she'd certainly come down from a
make-believe world of hero worship with a thud to face
her own limitations. Her gift, if you could call it that, of
being a mother hen was all that Rex and Rachel needed
of her.

The bag holding her ballet slippers slapped against her
knee as she went down the outdoor hillside steps. The
ache in her throat and the extremity of disappointment
and disillusionment were more insistent now that she was
alone in the privacy of a shrouding evening fog, the
redolent pungency of the old pepper tree, the familiar
blasts of the fog horns. She almost bumped into a figure
waiting for her at the street level.

"Hi! Lefty. Betts told me you were here for a lesson,
so I thought I'd pick you up." Walt's big, solid hand
closed on hers. They walked across the street to his
jalopy.

"It was nice of you to come." Cathy straightened her
shoulders. She tried to make her voice light, normal.

"Gee, it's good to have you back. And was I glad when
Betts told me that Danny and all the kids are O.K. at
camp." He paused a moment before starting the car.
"There's something I've been wanting to tell you about
my job. The guy who owns the place had a talk with
me. He wants some young, enterprising blood to go in
with him—more or less take over in another year so he
can open a branch riding academy at Redwood City."

"Perhaps it would be a good opportunity," she commented.

"It'll just mean being a glorified stable boy for a while, but there's a real chance for advancement later on."

"But Walt," Cathy started, suddenly aware of what he was really talking about, "you're not interested in horses or a riding school."

"Gosh, no! I've got college and all kinds of other fish to fry. That's what I told him. But I've been thinking ever since—there's your cousin Rick."

"Being a glorified stable boy isn't exactly like owning your own show horse."

"True," Walt conceded, "but it's a crime to work at anything you hate as much as he hates that bank."

"At least he'd be working with horses," Cathy agreed.

"We can tell him about it."

They rode along quietly for a space, and then Cathy said, "Sometimes you have to face a situation that isn't exactly what you want. I had to do that today." Her voice was a little squeezed, but the whole story came out right from the beginning. "So it looks like I'll be a teacher, maybe, instead of a ballerina. At least, I'll have a chance to see how I like teaching." She finished on a long, indrawn breath that dispersed the last drift of her dream.

"So why not? Golly, Cathy, that other idea struck me right from the start as something that had you going up on the down escalator. I just couldn't see it. In fact, I was so doggone uneasy, so completely knocked for a loop when you sprang it that I couldn't leave that night. If you'd told me right away that afternoon when I brought the fish that it was Rex Emory, perhaps I wouldn't have been so steamed up."

Cathy's memory went fumbling back. "But I did tell you."

"No, you didn't. Not until I came back later that night. Right then I just couldn't figure who had handed you such a phony line, and I've got to admit that when you thought I was going home to clean the rest of my fish, I hung around the house a while, hoping to see who was coming."

Cathy gave a quick, questioning gasp. "Then you were the mysterious man in the bushes?"

"Yeah. I was Betts' diamond thief," Walt confessed a bit sheepishly. "Was my face red when I sneezed, and you called out from an upstairs window. That was the time I should have stepped out, but—" Halting for a stop signal, he threw her a hasty grin that covered his unfinished apology.

Cathy felt her lips curve in an effort at response. The car jolted forward, turning up Van Ness Avenue, where the street lights had just come on. There was a short silence that seemed to leave space for Cathy's own train of thought again. She said finally, "I guess I should be pretty thankful for this opportunity to help Rachel. Especially since it came to me with no effort, you might say."

"Or you might say," Walt told her, "that it happened because you offered to take care of her baby. You were doing something you could do, wanted to do, and knew needed doing. It was the real Cathy, and it put a whole train of motion into action."

Suddenly the long day's weariness drew Cathy's head back against the old, worn upholstery. With a great effort she asked conversationally, "How're you coming with prumonds?"

"Oh, that? Well, I found a couple of other brilliant master minds had hit on the same idea. Matter of fact, there's a department at U.C. that's done considerable research, with the net result that while prune pits are edible, the process of shelling them is too expensive to make it a commercial bet." He brought the little car to a bucking halt at the curb in front of Faith's house. "I'm really concentrating on my carburetor now; and I've got another idea, too."

Walt would always have another idea. He was unbeatable. Cathy's eyes traveled over the cowlick in the center of his crew cut, the firm, steady set of his generous mouth, the big tanned nobleness of his features. But the tears of weariness, disillusionment, and frustration were so near the surface now that Cathy thought only of getting away. She gave the car door the sharp little slam that was the only way to make it close. "I'll say say good-by here." She bit her lip.

Walt leaned out the window. "O.K. I'll just watch till you get in." Their eyes met and held. "Golly, Lefty, it's going to be good to have you home again Monday. And I'm sure hoping you'll have a minute to come on over to the workshop."

Cathy nodded. "Of course I will." She started up the walk, surprised by the pressure of longing for home, for Dad, for all the hullabaloo of the children, Mee Chow, everybody and everything loved and known, including the gap in the hedge where she'd run through to Walt's basement workshop for years. She waved then from the top step, heard his little car clatter off.

Had it been only two weeks since she'd left home? So many new worlds had opened up. She wondered vaguely, tiredly where she'd been all her seventeen years less one day, not to have noticed how people really acted and thought. Her entire circle had become individuals with new dimensions—Gerry, Faith, Rick, Grandma, the children, Cora, Rex, Rachel, Walt—and herself.

In the early summer darkness, cheek pressed against the rough pink brick of the house, the stinging tears came at last. She looked at the Cathy who had taken a brief journey into another realm and had now returned. Returned to what? To the down-to-earth status of an in-between-ish person, she decided forlornly.

But couldn't she still set her sights high? Couldn't she be, if she wanted to, one of the very best teachers? There was expansive relief now in feeling smoothed out again. An expansive thrust of happiness in thinking that she and Rex would become real friends. Working with Rachel was going to be fun, exciting, a bridge to a new world.

That other Cathy had been struggling with a heavy lopsidedness of doubt and an uncertainty out of all proportion to the brief moments of rapture when she thought of Rex. Suddenly in the middle of all this she saw Gerry's face, the vibrancy, the enthusiastic acceptance of her new plans that she knew she'd find there. How proud she'd be to take Rex and Rachel to visit Gerry at her apartment! And how proud to have Gerry go with her to visit a class where she'd be Rachel's assistant!

Cathy turned, mystified by the long, low lines of the foreign car stopping out front, from which the tall, distinguished figure of a man emerged. She found herself dashing breathlessly down the walk. "Uncle Pat!"

"Is this—Cathy?" The low-voiced question was accompanied by his arms closing about her, holding her tight—wordlessly tight—providing the last bit of balm needed around her heart and reuniting her with all the comfort of home.

Even as she stood there a miraculous flash of intuition told her that she was doing the same for him. Gradually then he held her off to search her young, uplifted face. His big handkerchief wiped away the last tears she hadn't bothered to brush off. The astonishing discovery of their mutual emotion made it easy to say in explanation, "I thought I wanted something I didn't at all. It hurt to find out—but now I know just where I belong."

Their sighs melted together. "I understand." His hands gripped her slim shoulders affectionately; his voice was gravely tender. "That's exactly what happened to me."

Their smiles seemed to spring out at the same instant, too. "Oh, come on in," Cathy urged. "Everyone's so anxious to see you, so glad to have you home."

"Everyone?" Cathy heard his breath catch. Following his glance she looked up to Faith's room. The light was on, and there, clearly visible through the glass of the French windows that opened on the little balcony was the Paris hatbox on Faith's dressing table.

"Everyone," Cathy repeated with emphasis. She caught the tremor of joy that ran through him, the quickening of anticipation in the air. Her own happiness matched his—uprushing, outspreading. They took a step forward together, and that was when she thought of the phrase Grandma had used describing him—"the wild-eyed Irishman."

Almost as though reading her thoughts, he turned then, looking straight at her. Cathy saw that if there had ever been a time when his eyes were wild, it was different now. Because his eyes were just full of love.